I'LL GET YOU YET

The Steve Ashe Series

I'll Get You Yet
I Like It Tough
Blow Out My Torch
Die on Easy Street

I'LL GET YOU YET

JAMES HOWARD

CUTTING EDGE

ISBN-13: 978-1-7344295-3-4

Published by
Cutting Edge Publishing LLC
PO Box 8212
Calabasas, CA 91372

CHAPTER ONE

The big Mack ground westward through the chill night, eighteen tires crunching a dry powder of snow against the highway. Behind the cab were two trailers, carrying Steve's last link with Neon City—a load of eighty miles of fine glass tubing bent into shapes that would come aflame to advertise bars, cleaning shops, roller-coasters, hot dog Stands and mortuaries. He was thinking of this as he rode. He was thinking of a lot of things. He slid a cigarette between his lips and lighted it, then passed it over to Scotty who was tooling the heavy truck down the trail.

"Thanks."

Steve lit a second cigarette for himself, took a long pull, and ground his shoulders deeper into the leather seat.

"Want some music, Steve? The old can is usually good this time of night."

"Why not? Try to find something nice and soft, will you Scotty? Guess I'm still a little hung-over."

"You sure were on a lulu. Celebratin' something?"

"You might call it that. I just got sick up to my ears and decided to light out. Neon's one place I didn't want to stay."

"Hell, you had a good job, didn't you?"

"I suppose so—in a way. But there isn't any good job for a reporter. Every town is a stinking piece of the jungle. It can look so pretty from a distance ... like a place you'd really like to live—but get real close to it and you begin to find all the filth. And it's always the same filth."

"I read a book once said something like that. 'The face of evil is the face of the world. At times it smiles, at times it snarls. It traps and it destroys, but even in its destruction…'"

"'It is the face of shame because it cannot destroy that wrought by the single smile of a man it seeks make victim.' I remember that," Steve said. "I didn't know you read stuff like that, Scotty."

The big man straightened in his seat, looking out beyond the ribbons of light ahead of the truck. "I like it," he said. "Just like I like pushin' this bolt-bucket. Books make you think, and a truck gives you time—nights and nights of time—to do that: thinking in." He glanced at Steve. "We'll be in Omaha in a couple of hours. Do you want to try and catch some sleep? Or do you want to coffee up at Carroll? That's the last good place in Iowa, at least here on 30 it is."

"I could use a cup. How far yet?"

"Fifteen, maybe twenty minutes." Scotty never estimated distance in miles. Always in time.

Steve settled back and took a long pull on his cigarette. The radio fit a soft passage of Brahms to the incessant mumble of the diesel and the chorus of tires on snow. Scott drove automatically, handling the twenty-three tons of truck and cargo as though it were an extension of himself. For him it was and had been for a long time. At forty, he had pushed trucks into every state in the union. When he was parted from his vehicle he grew restless and on edge. His homecomings he sought eagerly, impatiently, but three days seemed his limit. By that time the urge would be there again, and he would roll out of Neon for somewhere, his dormant power restored by the simple process of putting his name on the call-board.

"What did Ivy think when I called you for a hitch?" Steve asked.

"You know Ivy, Steve. After sixteen years with me she's not surprised by anything." Scotty grinned, thinking of his wife. "It was little Scott who blew his top. He didn't want 'Uncle Steve' to go away. Neither did Mary Alice. Those kids really got a crush on you."

"They're great kids."

"Someday I'm gonna quit drivin' so that I can spend some time with 'em. It's not right to be without a father most of the time. I think I'll take that terminal job. It doesn't pay as much, but we own our place clear and got some money put by … And it would be pretty good to be home."

"You're ahead of schedule, Scotty. You usually don't start talking about settling down until you're in-bound." Steve grinned to himself. He'd heard this kind of talk for nearly three years … the three years he had known Scott Traybert.

"I'm not kiddin', Steve. I'm gonna do it." Scotty spoke as if he believed it.

"Yeah, Scotty, I … Heads up, Scotty!"

The sedan, heading into the path of the huge trucks swerved madly. Scotty's reflex was sure and precise. His? right hand pumped the trailer brake lever and he took the shoulder with the twenty-three tons, but not quickly enough. The sedan skidded on the snow and slid into the second of the two trailers. Bouncing off, it skittered up the highway for nearly a hundred yards before its crushed rear wheel ground it to a stop. Scotty continued braking and got the huge freighter stopped.

Like shots from a clip-filed automatic, Scott and Steve were out of the cab, running back down the lonely highway to the disabled car. It was upright. Scotty's quick reflexes had saved it from a mangled death.

They reached the sedan. Slumped over the wheel was a woman. Steve tried to wrench the sprung door open. It wouldn't give. Scott laid his two hundred and forty pounds against the sill as Steve hauled on the handle. There was a sharp click as the lock-spring gave, and the snap of the top hinge. The door opened, dangling. Steve lifted the woman gently, easing her from the car.

When Steve was clear of the car with the woman in his arms, Scotty stepped up and wrenched the front seat from the sedan, putting it in front of the headlights. Gently as he could, Steve deposited her on the seat. It was then he saw her face, beaten and bloody.

"My God!" he said, "look at her face!"

"That little side-swipe didn't do that, Steve. She's been beaten, really worked over."

Steve scooped a handful of the dry snow into his handkerchief. He ripped open the hood of the disabled sedan and placed the handkerchief against the hot exhaust manifold until the snow melted. With the wet cloth he returned to the girl, knelt beside her, and began to bathe her throat and temples.

"Get her coat out of the car, will you, Scotty?"

The big man went to the car. "There's no coat here, Steve," he said. "There isn't anything but this." He returned, holding a snub-nosed revolver in his huge hand.

The woman began to moan, then stirred. She opened shock-glazed eyes and poured out a stream of Italian, mixed invective and prayer.

"It's all right, cara mia," Steve said, "It's all right now. Just relax and take it easy."

She struggled to a sitting position, brushing her hair from across her face. "I've got to get away! Let me go! I've got to get away!"

It was then that Steve recognized her. Across eleven years and in spite of a change of hair color, he recognized in the woman the young girl he had loved ... the girl he had almost worshipped.

"Vicki," he whispered. "Vicki Marotti ..."

CHAPTER TWO

She looked at him, the film of fear over her eyes breaking with recognition. "Steve! Steve Ashe! Oh, thank God." She tried to rise.

Steve took her shoulders in his hands and held her. "Don't try to move, Vicki. You've been in an accident. Just lie quietly. We'll get a doctor. It'll be all right."

"The truck. I remember. That didn't hurt me, Steve. I'm all right. But I've got to get away. They're after me. I've got to get away!"

"Who's after you, Vicki? The law?"

"No ... honest to God, Steve. I'm not running from the police. I'd like to run to the police. It's Carazzi. He's after me. I ran away from them in Denver. They caught up with me in Omaha. The ... they got Gina. I tried to tell. They knew about it before I even got past a desk sergeant. That's when I started running. In Omaha I dyed my hair and went to work in a grease joint. I worked three days—then I had callers. They held me for two days, right in my own hotel room. They ... did this." She lifted a weary hand toward her battered face. "Tonight they got drunk—both of them. One of them went out for another bottle, and the other one tried to ... he ..."

She broke for a moment. Steve put his hand on her shoulder again. She went on. "He ... he had his coat off, and had a gun in a shoulder holster. I played up to him," she shuddered, "until I could get my knee up. I grabbed the gun. I should have killed him, but I didn't. I hit him with the gun as he lay there moaning—then I ran. Just grabbed his wallet and gun and ran out of the hotel. I kept running down the street, clear across the bridge into Council

Bluffs. I saw their car—this one—at the curb in front of a bar. I got in the back and stayed down behind the seat. When the tall one came out he started back from Council to the hotel. I put the gun against the back of his neck and told him to drive out into the country. At the edge of town I made him stop. I slugged him and dumped him out, then I started driving—driving like hell!"

Scotty had gone back to the truck. He came back, firing a fusee some fifty yards behind the wrecked car. No lights stirred in the Iowa countryside. Not a car had passed.

"Where were you going, Vic?"

"Chicago. I was going to my brother Vince. He could hide me."

"Nobody knows where you are?"

"I don't think so. I dumped the tall guy on Route 6, then cut back into Council and up to Route 30."

"Scotty," Steve called, "is the truck marked up?"

"Nothin' I could see, Steve. I guess she just bounced off the duals and broke that wheel by pulling it across the concrete. There's not a mark on the trailer that I could see."

"Good! Here's where the troopers get an unsolved mystery."

"What do you mean?"

"Scotty, this girl's a friend … a good friend who's in trouble. I'm gonna help her. Can I count on you?"

"What you got in mind?"

"I want to take her with us, back to Denver."

An animal sound of panic showed in Vicki's voice. "Denver? I never want to see Denver again!"

"Vicki, honey, listen. If they could find you in Omaha in three days, what makes you think you'd have more chance anywhere than right under their noses?"

Scott broke in. "What are you drivin' at, Steve?" he asked. "You mean we don't report this smash?"

"That's right."

"You're crazy!"

"Maybe, but this car isn't gonna be claimed … at least not right away. This kid's life depends on your answer. Will you help?"

Scott looked at Vicki's face, reading the terror as well as the bruises. He swung his glance back to Steve. "O.K., I'll play."

"Can you walk, Vic?" Steve asked.

She rose, swaying and unsteady.

"Spit!" Steve snapped. She looked at him for a moment, uncomprehending. "Spit!" he repeated, "right here in the snow."

She spat. There was no blood.

"Does your belly hurt?"

"Only where those goons hammered it."

"Good. Now walk down and climb into that truck before some car comes along." She turned and started toward the truck. "Wait!" Steve said. "Give me that wallet you took."

She dug into the pocket of her blood-spattered waitress uniform and handed it to him. He riffled through it, extracted nine of the crisp bills and stuffed them into his pocket, leaving about sixty dollars in the wallet. He tossed the billfold into the crippled sedan, "Now get down there and into that truck."

Scotty stood beside him, puzzled.

"Let's get this heap off the road, Scotty," Steve said.

Four hundred and twenty pounds of manpower rocked the sedan twice. On the third heave it lay over on its side and slid down the embankment into the ditch. They turned and walked fast back toward the truck. Steve bent and scooped up the fusee that sizzled against the highway. It made a flat arc through the air and burned its way into the piled snow of the ditch to black out with a sputtering gurgle .lost in the sound of the heavy diesel getting under way.

"One thing puzzles me, Steve," Scott said as he dropped into high range and began whipping the truck along toward Carroll. "Why the hell did you leave that dough and wallet?"

"Just so the law will be looking for the wrong guy."

A mile behind them the prairie wind was brushing off their tracks, using the dry powdery snow for sweeping compound.

CHAPTER THREE

Vicki Marotti slumped in the huge truck seat and had a quiet set of hysterics. The ground-in terror of the past days—the force of which had driven her to fight, dry-eyed and coldly raging—was withdrawn. The release from tension was more than her fear-addicted nervous system could take. Like a narcotics addict in withdrawal, she began to shake. Between fluttering breath and streaming tears, she shook herself upright and sobbed out her story.

"I was working at a bar across from the Mile High Track last summer. Just about paying the rent with the job and not much more. That's when I first met Carazzi. He was just another guy playing the circuit as far as I was concerned. He looked well heeled, and, well, he's good looking." Her voice cut a circle of air from around a curse and let it fall, hard. "The first notice I took of him was when he sent over a request slip. He asked if I could play any of Handel's Water Music, Imagine that! It made me sore, it always has ... the way some jerks still think that a girl at a bar Hammond is automatically out in left field when a classic is requested. I was so mad that I gave it to him, a twenty-seven-minute treatment." She paused and looked from Steve to Scotty. "Isn't this silly?" she asked. "The way I'm telling it?"

"It's all right, honey. We've got all the time in the world. You tell it just the way you want to."

"But it's so stupid. Here I sit on top of a volcano and all I can think of or talk about is how I felt about the way a guy asked for music eight months ago."

"Maybe it's easier, running it down from the beginning," Steve said. He lit a cigarette for her. She took it and put it between her battered lips.

"Thanks. Well, when I played the Handel, I gave it all the touch I had. It was good—concert good."

"Just say you played it. I know that's damned good." "When I finished, he came over. He gave me a hundred dollars. I'd had him figured for just another drunk trying to show off. He wasn't. He never drinks. Then he asked to take me home. I wish to hell I'd spit in his face—but I didn't. I didn't go home with him that night, either. But a couple of nights later, I did."

"He gave you a rough time?"

"Rough? He gave me the time of my life. The full treatment, dinner dates, presents … the works. In a week Dan Barton called me. He told me he had me booked at the Shirley—four hours a night for one-fifty. Very neat, wasn't it?"

"No more than you deserve."

"But more than I've made as a musician since San Francisco. Anyhow, to make a long story short, I went for it."

"And him."

"And him, the son-of-a—!"

"Still got him in your craw?" Steve broke in.

"Not any more. I'd like to spill his brains all over Carson Avenue."

"What made the change?" Steve asked, thinking to himself that whatever had turned Vicki against Carazzi, she still wanted him. The kind of hate she was spitting out couldn't succeed an affair without some hangover of desire, regardless of what had happened. The thought depressed him.

"We'd been together in an apartment out in the Heights for about five months when I began putting things together. He had a lot of Denver in his hip-pocket. That didn't bother me. But when I found out that he was more than a gambler —that he shaped up the narcotics and white-slave trade for the whole area from Santa

Fe to Helena—it turned my stomach. I wanted out." She paused, and took à long pull on the cigarette.

Steve didn't push for her to go on. They sat there for a long moment, staring ahead through the windshield with its reflected three red spots from the three cigarettes. Vicki went on.

"I'm no lily white, Steve. I haven't been for more years than I want to remember. But that racket—that's too much for me. I packed up and moved out. A week later I found myself looking for a job again. I also found that nobody in Denver wanted an organist, pianist or what have you. At least they didn't want me, not for long. I had three jobs inside of a week, and after them—nothing. But he wasn't done. The outfit that held the mortgage on my folks' place out in Boulder tried to foreclose. I had enough saved to stop that—it's clear now. He told me that no woman, or man either, could take a walk on him without getting hurt. I got hurt. I could take it. I took all of it, until he got Gina."

"Gina? She's just a kid!"

"She was a kid. She's an old woman now. She's had seventeen birthdays and she's a million years old."

"What happened?" Steve found his fists clenched and his nails biting into his palm. He forced his fingers to relax.

"He got a pretty boy, one I didn't know. The guy played her all the way, taught her all the things about men I'd sworn weren't going to happen to her. They turned her into a round-heeled little tramp, just because she was my sister. When they had made a mink of her, they got her on narcotics." Vicki shuddered at the word. "When they knew she was hooked deep—too deep to want to get out of it—they found me and told me the whole story. That miserable Carazzi told me himself. He asked me what house he should put her in. I went absolutely crazy. I tore into him. I got my nails down his face just once, and then somebody hit me. I woke up in an alley behind some bar with these."

Vicki rolled up her sleeves and took Steve's hand in hers. She stroked it down her inner arm. The scars of poorly administered hypodermics were like festering pimples.

"My God," Steve breathed. "The filthy... He broke off, speechless.

"I guess they thought they'd killed me. They knew if I wasn't dead I'd be hooked and have to have it. I'd been kept unconscious for eleven days. My other arm is just like this one, and my belly and legs are scarred, too. They'd given me about fifty shots to make sure I was hooked."

Scotty cracked the wind-wing slightly to clear the smoke out of the truck-cab. He didn't know how to say it, but he had to ask.

"Are you still hooked?"

"No. I'm not. When I found out what they had done, I knew I had to get out of it, somehow. I hitchhiked down to Palmer and went out to the old stable. I put myself in the tack room, padlocked the door, and slid the key out under it. If I could have, I'd have killed myself." Vicki shuddered as if she had drawn her nails across a blackboard. She was dry-eyed now, and flamed again as she went on with her narrative.

"I stayed there four days. By then I had them beaten and I knew it. I wanted the stuff so bad I'd have cut off • an arm for just one jolt, but I had them whipped. I found an old spur and whittled around the lock with it until the hasp came off. That took the last two days. I was really silly when I put myself in there alone. I could have died there and not have been found till April or May when they bring the horses in for the summer. I wasn't thinking of anything but beating them when I locked myself in. I guess I was crazy."

Scotty had been driving quietly, listening to it all. Except for the one question he had said nothing. He had a remarkable power to keep his mouth shut and listen, but even the most remarkable of quiet men finds some things to which he must respond. He breathed it softly, almost to himself. "I think you were magnificent."

Steve found nothing that he could trust himself to say. Vicki went on as if she hadn't heard. "I got back to Denver. I'd taken off my clothes when I put myself in there—so that I couldn't take them and tear them up. They'd hung out fairly straight. I just wrapped up in some filthy old saddle-blankets to get warm. Anyhow, I dressed, and washed my face in the lake after I got out. I robbed a bait box and ate some raw fish. It made me sick but I kept them down. Then I hitched back. It's kind of foggy. I went to my apartment. The janitor let me in—they'd taken my purse, keys, everything. The place had been gone over with a comb, but nothing was missing. I cleaned up, drank about a quart of milk with some bourbon in it. I took my car and started for Lieutenant Morrow's office. When I got to headquarters, Larry Kenner and Jack...I don't know his last name...they were waiting for me, talking to the desk sergeant. They gave me a big hello, like old friends, and told me that Mario wanted to see me. I knew they'd cut me down if I said I wouldn't go. Probably they would kill the sergeant too. But I knew one other thing. They couldn't refuse to allow me to go to the powder room in front of the sergeant. I went in—and out the window. I made it to my car just as they came out the door. I got out of there quick. I only made one stop—at Jimmy Mahon's house. I tapped him for thirty bucks. It was every dime the guy had. Then I lit out."

She accepted another cigarette. "I got to Lincoln and pitched the car to a used car lot. Then I took a bus into Omaha. I got my hair dyed brown, went to a cheap optometrist who managed to find that I needed glasses, and then I went job hunting. I knew better than to try to work a club. I took a job as a waitress in a hamburger joint. They found me in exactly three days. You know the rest of it."

"How could they find you so damned soon?" Steve asked. "Did you tell anyone in Denver where you were going? Jimmy Mahon or anybody?"

"No."

Scotty had the next question. "Did you go into any of the hot spots in Omaha?"

"No. That would be the first place they'd have looked. I knew better than to do that. All that I can figure is that the word went out."

"Where was the beauty shop where you had the changeover?" Steve fired the question quickly.

"A cheap one, right across from the bus station. I didn't want the job to look too good. I figured that looking hard, with the weight I'd lost, and glasses—I thought that would make it tougher for them. Tough!" she said bitterly. "It was almost like I'd mailed out change-of-address cards."

"All right, honey. Now think." Steve took a pencil from his pocket, reached over and tripped the map-light switch, then pulled an envelope from his inside coat pocket and began to write. "I want the names of everyone you can remember seeing since you left that tack-room. Everyone you saw or talked to."

He had a list of nine persons in Denver, the beauty shop and optometrist's locations, the address of the restaurant where Vicki had worked and the hotel where she had lived in Omaha, when Scotty broke in again.

"Well, we didn't stop at the good joint in Carroll, but we're coming to Ulcer Gulch about five minutes down the road. We better coffee up, I think." He turned toward Vicki. "You'd better stay in the truck. We'll bring you out somethin'. Keep down flat on the seat."

CHAPTER FOUR

Scotty shoved the truck off the road onto the huge drive of the truck stop, pulled past the gasoline pumps and into the shadows nearly one hundred yards from the red-and-white restaurant building. After spreading his topcoat over Vicki, Steve slid out of the truck on the right side. Together with Scotty he walked briskly toward the building, shivering a little from the cold air.

"Never heard anything quite like that," Scotty said. "I thought I'd seen every kind of scum that was, but to keep a girl hopped up until she was an addict—I hope somebody cuts their guts out."

Steve didn't answer him. He didn't mention the situation until they were in the diner, standing against the oil burning heater along the end wall of the building. Then he opened up and gave Traybert the whole story. Eleven years before, when Steve was attending the University, he had lived at the Marottis'. Vicki had taken the place of sister, sweetheart, and teacher. It was Vicki who had given him an appreciation of music and the arts, she who had taught him to let go and live. She was two years younger than he, but until the war had come along to kick him out of his rut, he was simply a rancher's son, poorer than most, and naïve to the point of non-belief in evil. To Steve, range tough, and a social fumbler, she had been the center of the world, beautiful and unattainable. Seeing her like this had hit him where he lived ... hit him hard and brought back that well-remembered tight core of pain he always felt when he wondered if he could ever measure up to his idea of a man. The measuring up was the spring that drove him—made him try anything to prove himself, over and over. Any hurt was pain, but more than that it was challenge. He was near to realizing this when Scotty broke in.

"Everybody's got a woman like that, somewhere," Scotty said as Steve finished his story. "You never really get over them."

"The Marottis were a second family to me, Scotty. Gina is the sort of a kid sister that you never . get over, either. She was such a beautiful child that everyone just spoiled her rotten. You just couldn't help yourself. She was only six when I left. I'd told her stories, put her to bed at night, taken her into Denver on trips to the zoo. It's hard to talk about her, too. I've seen her a couple of times since I came back from overseas. I went to Boulder a few times, hoping to find Vicki, I suppose. Never did have it timed right, though. Vicki was always playing in some other city and when she was there, I was someplace else. Gina was always around, though. Even back in '46, when she wasn't quite eleven, you could see that she was going to be beautiful. In '52 when I was back, she took my breath away … just to look at her. She's a spoiled little teaser … she took great delight in ruining her current beau's day by making me take her to the high-school hangout for a malt. I wasn't 'Uncle Steve' then. I was her 'very special friend, Mr. Steven Ashe of the *Neon City News*. She rubbed his face in it. He'd have gladly broken me in half if I'd said 'boo!' At least he'd have tried to."

"Every girl goes through that stage."

"For all her life?"

The counterman put an end to the conversation by emerging from the tiny kitchen with two platters of paper-thin, ham and slightly grey eggs. They ate silently, ordered sandwiches and a quart of coffee to take out. They paid the bill and left, walking silently. There was nothing more to say.

It was five-thirty when the truck bulled its way into the Omaha suburbs. The weathered shacks along the route were lighted just enough for visibility by a cold-breaking dawn and not enough to show their raw prairie squalor.

"Scotty," Steve said, "I think I've got it figured." Nearly an hour had passed since either of them had spoken. Vicki was sleeping between them, wrapped in Steve's topcoat.

"Yeah?" the quiet mountain of flesh rumbled. "How'd they do it?"

"Not that, that I can't figure. I mean I know what we can do with Vicki for a little while."

"Go on."

"Can I take you a hundred or so miles out of your way?"

"Hell, yes. Why do you even ask?"

"The way it looks, she's gonna have to be out of sight for a couple of weeks. That beat-up face would cause talk anywhere, and there's always the chance that she'd slip and take some dope. She didn't have more than a shock cure. What I want you to do is take her to my folks' place outside Lamar. If you cut down to 50 South you can probably pick up most of the time between Manhattan and Pueblo. Maybe you'll even make Denver on time."

"That's no strain. Ole Gert'll do it." He patted the dash cowling of the heavy truck affectionately. "But how do I find your folks' place in Lamar?"

"You go on through Lamar, right on 50 South. About six miles over the bridge there's a fork in the trails, where 50 goes right. There'll be a grey '49 Plymouth four-door waiting for you at the Phillips station on the Junction point. The fellow driving will be my Dad. He'll know what to do—I'll phone him and fill him in on the whole story. He'll take Vicki with him, and she'll be safe ... both ways."

"You mean you aren't going on to Denver with me?"

"That's right. I've got to see if I can't get the hook-up here. I can figure how they thought it would be Omaha since she pitched her car in Lincoln, and Omaha is the nearest big town. What I'm going to try to do is find out how they spotted her to the exact location, when her whole appearance and personality had been so changed."

"You're liable to get your damned head knocked off, too. You know that, don't you?"

"Yeah." Steve's voice was quiet.

"Why don't you just stay out of it? Help her get away —that's enough."

"And what about Gina?"

"Send the law after her. Get her committed as an addict." The big man's worried frown was screened by the darkness of the cab, but his voice was naked with concern.

"Is that what you'd do, if you were me?"

"No, but then I'm a damned fool too."

Steve smiled. He stuck his hand into his pocket and pulled out the fifty-dollar bills he had taken from the wallet. He peeled off the top four bills. "Use one of these to buy distillate so your company won't have any charge slips that record you off your scheduled route. They might think you had been joy-riding. Get your load of fuel here, just like you were running Denver the regular way, and then pay cash for everything you need while you're off the regular trails. Give Vicki the rest of the money when she wakes up. Tell her to do exactly what my old man says, and not to contact anyone till she hears from me. You can also tell her that I owe her two-fifty. I'm nearly broke and I've got to be able to live without going to work."

"O.K. Steve—anything else?"

"Not that I know of. I'll drop at the first big boulevard where I can catch a bus."

"That's about six blocks."

Steve reached behind him and wrestled his beat-up gladstone bag off the sleeper shelf. Scott crossed the boulevard, then laid the truck over to the curb. He gently lifted Steve's coat from the sleeping girl and replaced it with his own heavy mackinaw. Vicki stirred slightly.

"It's all right, honey," Scott purred, "Go ahead and sleep."

Steve reached for the door handle. He felt Scotty's hand on his shoulder. He looked back across the cab at his friend.

"Steve," Scott said, "this might come in handy." He handed over the snub-nosed banker's special he had taken from the wrecked sedan. Steve grasped his big hand for a moment and looked at him, then he bent and kissed Vicki gently. He turned away and opened the door without looking back. He dropped the gun into his suitcoat pocket and. stepped off the fender plate onto the Omaha sidewalk.

CHAPTER FIVE

Steve waited momentarily on the sidewalk as the truck slid away from the curb. The little running lights blinked once as Scotty gave the highway farewell. The situation of the last three hours was still revolving in Steve's mind as rapidly as its impact was revolving in his belly. He slid into the topcoat, extracted gloves from its pocket, and picked up his valise. Come what might, he was committed now. It was a feeling he had known before. It was the feeling he had known when breaking a horse, flying a combat mission, fighting, or going after a story. His breathing was uneven and sweat oozed onto his forehead. He was afraid, scared more of failing himself than of danger. Inside his gloves his palms felt sticky. He pulled up the topcoat collar to shield himself from the biting wind and walked rapidly, trying not to think about the feelings bouncing up out of his body.

Omaha slept on like a tired prostitute, with only. minor stirrings in the deep-buried sinew of the prairie town. Here and there a kitchen light snapped on, a sleepy eye against the steadily bleaching sky. It was that strange time between dark and daylight when workers and their tired wives activate themselves, collectively becoming a town, a labor force, a stream of commuters, the muscles and entrails of a city.

The green and white bus hauled itself reluctantly up to the curb, wheezing against the cold and the relentlessness of its driver. Steve climbed aboard.

"Fare?" Steve asked.

"Fifteen," the driver said. "Fi' cents back if you get off in the zone."

Steve dropped a dime into the maw of the coin-box, and fumbled for a nickel. He found one after a little time and let it rattle in pursuit of the dime. The driver stared at him for an insolent moment, noticing the wrinkled topcoat and the angry, unshaven face. Mentally he classified Steve as a highway bum. No local man would have had to ask the fare. On the prairie all strangers are judged on sight.

Steve stared back until the driver looked away, then he turned and walked back into the bus. Only one suburban rider had preceded him on board … a tired-looking little man who slouched against the window and wrestled with his dyspepsia.

On the sixty-block ride to the downtown area, Steve occupied himself with pouring over the names and addresses he had scribbled on the envelope. As they passed the garish Corn Palace, he was satisfied that he had them memorized. He tore the envelope into tiny pieces and ground the pieces into the snow-wet floor.

A few blocks later the driver called the Union Station stop. Steve pulled the bell cord and stepped into the door well at the rear of the bus. The coach shuddered to the stop and hissed its doors open. Steve dropped onto the street, the chill wind pushing him toward the station.

Six-fifteen in the morning is a time when there are few places where soap and hot water are available, but a Union Pacific Terminal is one of them. Steve strode across the terrazzo to the washroom. It was hot and stuffy. He wadded a paper towel into the drain of the cleanest of the long line of washbowls. From the Gladstone bag, he extracted a plastic travel box containing razor, soap, brush and washcloth. He stripped to the waist, piling his clothes atop the wrinkled topcoat on the vault-like window ledge.

While he scrubbed and shaved himself, a train entered the station with a dyspeptic cough and regurgitated its contents into the waiting rooms. The washroom swelled with its periodic cargo. They came, stared at the travel-weary man's total unconcern and his adept use of the glittering straight edge razor, then left. Momentarily they carried on them the imprint of raw masculinity, but they quickly forgot him.

The flowing and ebbing tide of flesh was of no concern to Steve Ashe. At the moment he was concerned only with devising an approach to the beauty shop Vicki had visited. He could conceive of no immediate plan to get information about it quickly. His anger gave him a desperate sense of urgency, and he boiled inwardly with the frustration of delay.

The last of the human tide was ebbing from the room. A rather florid-looking man was slowly washing his soft, delicate, and well-manicured hands.

The idea hit Steve then. He knew how to proceed.

Steve dressed rapidly, pulling a clean shirt from the bag, putting on the first tie his neck had known since he had started the binge in Neon City four days before.

"Funny," he said to himself. "It's so simple I should have thought of it. All I need is a manicure."

CHAPTER SIX

I t was eight-twenty when Steve arrived at the bus station. He had made only one stop in the squalid blocks that are generated between railway stations and the downtown areas of any city. Generated like scabbed-over stores to house the shops and people that never quite made it downtown and never quite made it out of town either. That one stop had been at a cheap cleaning store where the sight of an unexpected five dollars had put a fat Greek to the task of giving Steve a well-pressed look of his own. The chill air in his lungs and the chance to use his body in the walk toward town had finished off the last traces of the hangover Steve had brought to Omaha.

It had seemed to him that the bus station was the logical place to start his search for information. Vicki had arrived by bus, and it seemed possible that a spotter team worked the terminals to watch for fingered victims. She hadn't changed her appearance until after her arrival. The simple explanation would be the bus terminal.

He circulated through the station for nearly two hours. In those two hours he had collected only a high gloss on his shoes, a half-read magazine, and a coffee-soured stomach. Eight busses had arrived, but nobody loitered for more than two arrivals. The people Steve watched were there either to meet disembarking passengers, or to board one of the busses. He noticed the station employees particularly. At no time did any one of them remain in a position where all arriving passengers could be observed.

"I suppose it's possible that spotters work only when they know somebody's running," Steve mused to himself. He made himself a mental promise to check that hypothesis if his other leads took him nowhere. It was possible that he had missed, or even that spotters would work a shift-off so smoothly that it could pass unnoticed. "That kind of checking would take time," he thought, "I'll work all the other angles first."

His watch pointed to ten-thirty. "Good time for a manicure," he mumbled … "Just the right time." He chuckled to himself as he made his way to the street.

The Powder Box was the only beauty shop in the block opposite the bus station. Steve walked slowly past the shop. Its discreet draperies, its slightly worn leather-quilted door attempted to pretend that the Powder Box was a special haunt of the smart woman. But the open arch connecting it with the barber shop next door belied the pretense and made things easier for Steve. He could have a haircut and look over the beauty shop. It seemed likely that the manicure service of the barber shop was drawn from the staff of the Powder Box.

He entered the barber shop and took a chair to wait his turn. Through the archway he had a fair view of the inside of the beauty parlor. Three women customers were gathered into the hive-like dryers near the front of the shop. Further back, four operators stood with hands on hips or lounged on the hip-high work counters in front of the long mirrors. In the five minutes Steve waited, the organization of the women became evident. The tall redhead left no doubt that she was in charge.

When Steve's turn came, he spoke to the barber who crossed to the archway and called the redhead. She strolled into the barber shop, provocativeness in her walk.

"Yes sir, a manicure?"

"That's right, but not while I'm in the chair. I'll come over when I'm finished, Is that all right?"

"Of course," she said. "We have tables just through the archway."

"I'm quite particular. Are you the manager?"

"I'm the owner. I'm sure that we can please you."

"I'm sure that you could." The double entendre did not pass unnoticed. It was sufficient to insure that the lady would see to this customer personally.

For thirty minutes after leaving the barber chair, Steve endured the torture of a deliberately prolonged manicure. During this time he eased himself into the role of a lover of beauty, appealing to the snobbery he found just below her surface. The Steve Ashe who emerged was something of an artistic dilettante, but a vitally masculine one. It was very easy to persuade the woman to have luncheon with him.

The luncheon was excellently planned. In the two hours before Steve returned to the beauty shop he had checked the better of the downtown hotels until he found the right decor and the string quartet. And when he called for the redhead, his appreciation of her vivid green dress ("how striking with your lovely hair") was calculated to charm her.

In the dining room Steve took a tiny card from his handkerchief pocket, made a check mark on it, and gave it to the headwaiter. As the table waiter took their order, the card bore fruit—or rather flowers. The headwaiter brought a corsage of small white camellias to the table. With a courtly flourish Steve presented it to his guest.

She let a heavy-lidded languorous gaze find him appreciatively. "Beautiful," she murmured, "and in such perfect taste. But what if I had shown up in winter white?"

"I must confess it was subterfuge," he chuckled. "Look!" From his pocket he extracted four other cards, each bearing his name and the name of a different kind of flower. Under the names were written the sizes, small, medium, and large.

"Do you always carry these?" she inquired.

"No. I wrote them this morning. But somehow I knew it would be camellias. I pride myself that I am rarely mistaken in an immediate impression of people. You are camellias."

The waiter interrupted the scene. Steve scarcely glanced at the menu. He ordered for both of them, consulting her only for specific dislikes. When the waiter had slunk back to that netherworld from which hotel dining rooms fetch their food, the conversation resumed.

"You are quite a remarkable man. Here I am having lunch with you and I don't even know your name."

"It's Blair. Curtis Blair." Steve lied automatically.

"Somehow it fits. Let me check my impressions. You do something creative—paint or sculpt."

"You're quite close, actually. I'm a writer, of sorts." Steve smiled inwardly. The writing he did was primarily the batting out of stories on love-nest slayings or gory accidents for the thrill-starved readers of second-rate daily papers.

She glanced at the well-tailored suit and topcoat. They had taken more than a month's wages from Steve in his periodic sprees of buying only the best. "And somewhat successful," she added.

"It's a living."

"You came here to write."

"I haven't been able to write for days." Again Steve smiled to himself, thinking of the recent binge. "I have a character in a situation, and frankly I don't know just what to do. I fear that I'll be in for a long period of research."

Steve was banking on the first feminine wile—that of getting a man to discuss his problems. He wasn't disappointed. "Just what kind of a situation?" she said.

"One that you could help with, I imagine. In the situation a young woman is trying to put her past behind her. She wants to change everything about herself, and to change entirely. I suppose it would be as complete as her hair color, style of dress, speech, habits—everything. I'm afraid I just don't know enough about women."

"This I doubt," she smiled.

"No, truly I don't. What would be a woman's idea of changing herself?"

"What kind of woman?"

"Blonde…blonde and very beautiful, the ultimate of femininity and sophistication. I picture her after the changes as being rather dowdy and hard-looking. Your techniques of beauty in reverse, I suppose. What would that kind of woman do to change?"

She thought a moment. "She'd probably start with a hair dye…not too good a hair dye. Then she would simply pick the make-up which would go with her new hair color."

Steve watched her closely as she spoke. There was no indication that the question had disturbed her. To further allay suspicion, the words she was saying as he redirected his attention to her words put him even more at ease.

"As a matter of fact," she was saying, "a situation very similar to yours came up at the shop last week. An extremely attractive young blonde came in. She took our cheapest hair dye. I didn't think anything of it until she opened her purse to pay. It was not the lack of money that led her to take the low-priced treatment. She had quite a bit in the bag."

"Was she one of your regular customers?"

"No, she had just walked in off the street."

"What exactly did you do for her?"

"I can't remember—just the recoloring and then we did sell her some brownette cosmetics, I think."

"Has she come back?"

"No. I only saw her once. Very strange that you should have such a situation. I hadn't even thought of her since she left the shop—but now, in view of what you said…" She paused a minute, and a tiny frown furrowed her brow between the perfectly drawn eyebrows. "I do believe that she was deliberately trying to make herself less attractive," she added.

"Or less noticeable, I suppose. Heavens, that whole process seems simple enough. I can't imagine why I should have considered it difficult."

"The other things would be more difficult, I imagine. Changing personality and habits is not easy. At least I shouldn't think so. I haven't the faintest idea how she would go about doing that."

It was obvious to Steve that the syndicate hadn't traced Vicki through the beauty shop. He dismissed the whole topic for the pleasant banalities of the luncheon table. The waiter had reappeared, and the food was excellent.

When the luncheon was completed, and the string quartet had followed the unionized dictates of their contracted conscience, the woman did not go back to the beauty shop. At five-thirty as he was leaving her apartment, she had just one more comment.

"By the way," she murmured lazily, "my name is Marie."

CHAPTER SEVEN

The metal of the public locker clicked as the key released the door. Steve swung the gladstone bag out of the hole, left the station and took a cab back to the uptown district. At a moderately good hotel he had found while surveying for luncheon atmosphere, he registered under the name he had given Marie—Curtis Blair. He inquired for commercial rates by the week, called them satisfactory, and asked to have a boy sent up shortly for some valuables he wanted to have put in the hotel safe. The suave and impeccable manager was polite—in a bored, uninterested and entirely professional manner. Steve felt slightly uncomfortable, but he felt this would be the right place to cut his ties with the past, at least emptying his identity into a hotel safe might do this for him.

In his room he went over the few possessions he had brought with him. He removed all identification from the bag, labels from his clothing, cards, papers, and envelopes from his wallet. He sealed these inside a large hotel envelope. He folded two pairs of socks and two changes of shorts into small wads and stuck them into his topcoat pockets. Between the pages of an evening paper he had picked up in the lobby, he slipped two shirts and another tie. The flat, compact shaving kit slipped into one suitcoat pocket. He checked the cylinder of the gun and slipped it into the other. Satisfied that he had nothing traceable which was not in the envelope, he called the desk and asked for the bellboy. When the boy had collected his tip and disappeared, Steve walked down the stairs to the lobby, turned in his key, and walked out into the February evening.

A few moments of walking brought him to a pawnshop he had noticed during the day. He picked out a suitcase of good quality but travel-battered appearance and unloaded his pockets into it. A sport coat that had seen better days was added from the used garment rack. At the top of the pile he added the two shirts. The broker buried his nose in the ledgers to establish the reasonable price of what the traffic would bear.

"Twenty-eight dollars, according to the loans made."

Steve said nothing, but quietly began to unpack the bag. "… but of course, I have had the merchandise a long time, so I'm willing I should take a slight loss to get it off my hands." It was more of a question than a declaration.

"Twelve bucks."

"Impossible! If you were my own brother …"

"Twelve," said Steve, continuing with unloading the bag onto the counter.

"Let us say eighteen."

Steve took the sport coat back to the used garment rack, hung it neatly on a hanger, and returned to the counter. He stuffed the wadded socks and shorts back into his topcoat pocket.

"Fifteen?" the little fat man asked.

"It's robbery, but I need the goods." Steve dropped a five -and a ten on the counter, rescued the sport coat, and repacked the bag.

"I haven't made a nickel all day," the little man whined.

Steve dug into his pants pocket. A five-cent piece spun and racketed on the counter as he closed the door behind him.

Three doors down the street a small job-print shop bore a sign on the front door which said "Closed." Steve saw light in the back room, and watched until he saw a pressman cross to a lay-out table. He rapped at the door. The man looked up, then pointed to the sign. Steve rapped again. Reluctantly the man came to the door.

"We're closed!" he yelled through the glass. "Can'tcha read?"

Steve pressed a bill against the window. The press operator raised an eyebrow—then motioned to the rear of the shop. Steve nodded and the man made a circling motion with his hand. "Back door!" he yelled.

Circling the building by way of a vacant lot and a dirty alley, Steve arrived at the rear door of the shop. The man was standing in the doorway, his stained fingers against the jamb.

"What was it you wanted, friend?" he asked.

"I need a very little job done, tonight."

"You're out'a your mind. I can't take jobs without the boss puts the O.K. on 'em."

"Well, it really isn't much, and I'll pay."

"So for ten lousy bucks I should stick my neck out?"

"I had more than ten in mind. If I could wait till morning I could get the whole job for four."

"What's so special about tonight?" The pressman put his ink-stained hand in motion, bringing it from the door jamb to his shirt pocket long enough to extract a cigarette. He lit it and spit out a stream of blue-grey smoke into the chill air. As soon as he had finished admiring the trail of rising smoke, he centered Steve in his stare again.

Steve matched the stare. "I got a guy to see. It might mean a good deal for me, but I lost the intro touch. All I need is three business cards, an indent blank—any common stock item—and a couple of letter headings. If you happen to have a DAV card, I can use one of them, too."

"So the law can come breathe at me? No deal."

"It's a fast twenty bucks, buddy. That's all I got. How about letting me show you what I want, then just saying yes or no?"

"Turn around." Steve turned, and inky hands patted over his arm-pits and hips. There were no bulges. "Gotta be careful who comes into the shop at night," he said, nodding Steve in.

Steve took a sheet of make-up scratch from the rack, laid it on the stone, and roughed in the business card forms. They bore a minimum of information, simply some Chicago racket names—Merchant's Underwriters, American Amusements, and Allardo Supply.

"This is what I want for the cards. The letterheads carry just two letters in the upper left corner on the forty-five, T R in script. I only need one of each. You can block 'em and make it in one run; then we'll cut them after they're on the board. The letterheads you can knock one at a time with your galley mallet—they don't have to be exact." He handed the man the proof sheet.

"For this I get twenty bucks? There must be a fast pitch goin' on somewhere."

"You get twenty for that one set, five minutes use of your typewriter, and my watching while you break the forms when you're done."

"Hell, I'd do that anyhow. I wouldn't take a chance on the boss askin' no questions. All black?"

"Letterheads in standard blue?"

"You got a deal," the man said. "What you want first?"

"Knock the letterheads … it'll save time if I'm typing while you set the other stuff."

An hour and ten minutes later, at the fringe of the business district, the man with the new identity of Curt Blair checked in at a cheap hotel. It was less than twenty-four hours since Vicki Marotti had fought for her life in the same hotel.

CHAPTER EIGHT

The Diegan Hotel was three floors of flea bag. It made a shabby try at respectability with a marble-faced desk in the old lobby and a brass plaque at shoulder height on the wall outside the revolving door. Behind the plaque and the desk lay another tired, dirty hotel. Behind the desk sagged another tired desk clerk, distinguishable from other deskmen in cheap hotels by the fact that he was enormous. His huge rolls of fat quivered like gelatin, and his red-rimmed eyes peered out at the world with a non-attached contempt. He was perhaps five or ten years on either side of fifty. His bulk made age impossible to estimate. He had the desolate look of a man who is forced to admit that he isn't going anywhere—without understanding that he never could. He fit the shabby, tired lobby, at home amid wilting rubber plants and worn plush.

He looked up at Steve as the new Curtis Blair sauntered up to the desk. The look was sour. Steve felt the man's eyes run down his body like two dirty drops of sweat.

"Yeah?" The word was as tired as the man.

"Gotta room with a bath?" Steve asked.

"Four a day, or twenty-five a week. In advance."

Steve slid his hand into his coat pocket and pulled out the long, expensive wallet. He opened it to extract a ten and two singles, making sure the clerk got a look at the bright corners of the fifties.

"If you're interested in entertainment..." he began.

"I'm interested in a clean room. That's all," Steve said as he signed the card.

The huge roll of fat shrugged some pillow-like portion of his shoulders, and let the heap of flesh that served him for a hand fall on the brass bell. The elevator boy deserted his post and came to the desk.

"Two-fifteen," the clerk said, flipping the key to the boy. The boy shot him a glance of undiluted hate and picked up Steve's bag. He wheeled without a word and retreated to the elevator. Steve followed and the car ground up the single flight past the mezzanine.

"Someday I'm gonna clobber that fat jerk," the boy said, almost to himself. He was lean and bitter with his twenty years of unfulfilled life.

"Don't let it throw you, kid. Maybe his wife pushes him too hard."

"That fat fruit? All he likes is his bottle and the boys." The elevator operator made an effete gesture with flexed wrist.

The car halted. They walked the few steps to the room. The boy put the key in the lock, opened the door, and went through motions of opening windows and checking the towel supply in the bath. When he came back into the room, Steve had closed the door and was sitting on the end of the bed. He had a five-dollar bill wound around his fingers. The kid looked at him quizzically.

"I want some information."

"Blonde, brunette, or redhead?"

"None. What time are you through here?"

"Eleven."

"I'll be at the diner four blocks down the street. Drop in and I'll match this for you, and maybe more." He ripped the five in half, and gave one piece of it to the boy. The kid looked at him narrowly, took the torn half of the bill and nodded. Then he left.

Steve took his first real bath in five days and dressed again. He put the gun in the bag under a shirt and sat down to relax with the papers he had packed in the bag. He looked over police and crime items especially, and with practiced eye. If he began to run out of money, he'd have to go to work somewhere, and news reporting was his trade. He decided that the Standard would be his first try. The police beat of a morning sheet would keep him circulating through the night hours. "Hope I don't need that long," he mused, "but I better put some lines out in a day or two, just in case."

It was ten-thirty when he rose from the chair. He again opened the bag and made sure the gun was only partially concealed. He slipped two of the letters he had typed into-a pocket of the bag, then wound a thread through the latch and closed the suitcase. He didn't expect action immediately, but he wanted the stage set. He left the room and used the stairs going down to the lobby. As he crossed the lobby, the clerk looked up from his chair behind the desk.

Steve pushed through the door and emerged into the street. It was cold, and the quarter moon looked like a banana thrown into the air. He looked at it for a moment, waiting for his eyes to adjust. Four blocks down the street was the diner. He looked the other way. About six blocks away was the bridge, and on the other side was Council Bluffs. Six blocks and one bridge-width away was a huge neon sign with the one word, Liquor.

He turned and walked back to the diner. He took a back booth and ordered coffee and a steak sandwich. Behind the counter, at the grill, was the man Vicki had called "Al." The place was nearly deserted. He had finished his sandwich and was on his second cup of coffee when the elevator boy walked in.

"Sit down," Steve said. "What'll you have?"

"Coffee, that's all." The waitress ambled off and returned with two more mugs. When she had left, the boy eyed Steve again. "All right, mister," he said, "what's your pitch?"

"Five days ago a woman checked into your hotel."

"Why not? It's a free country." The boy was sparring, trying to cope with the desperate, angry intensity which he saw filtering into Steve's eyes.

"Let's say she was my wife. I knew where she was, but I didn't want her found. She was found—found and beaten half to death in your hotel. She got home to me and told me she'd slugged her way out when one of the two guys went out for a bottle. I want those two guys." Steve's voice was a low, intense crackle. "I want those guys bad, and I want 'em quick."

"Honest to God, I don't know anything about nothin' like that."

"I didn't figure that you would, but the two guys held her for two days, right in that room. One of them would have been holdin' his groin and nursing his head today. Did you see 'em?"

"Do you know what room she was in?"

"She said it was two seventeen."

"You mean Miss Graves? Brown hair, glasses, kinda pretty? I wondered why I hadn't seen her for a couple of days. She came in a couple of nights ago with two guys. At that flea bag that ain't unusual. I saw the guys a couple of times the next day, but I didn't see her."

"Do you know the guys?"

"They're local. I seen 'em before. I don't know their names, but the black-haired one, they call him Curley, he shoots craps at Marelli's damned near every night. I seen him there lots of times. Once in a while I pick up a couple of extra bucks runnin' drinks to the table."

"How do you get into the joint?"

The slim youngster took a long look at Steve. Then he fished in his tunic pocket and came up with a card. It carried the single letter "M." "You just give this to the colored boy in the washroom. If you're cleared by the guy behind the mirror, you go through the can marked 'out of order.' I guess I better tell you, those guys are pretty rough."

"Tell me exactly what the two guys look like," Steve said. He questioned the kid about dress, habits, or anything which might pin down an identification. After a few minutes he had a fair picture of the men, plugging in everything that the kid had seen or could remember with the outline of information he had gotten from Vicki.

The bellhop looked up at him again. "Mister, I don't know what your beef really is, or even if she was your wife. But she was nice to me. I seen her workin' in this very joint last Thursday. I thought you'd oughta know."

Steve added a ten to the torn half of the five and dropped them in front of the kid. "How do I find Marelli's?" he asked.

"It's the first joint across the bridge, on the Iowa side."

"The joint with the big-sign you can see from here?"

"Yeah."

"Thanks." Steve rose and dropped a dollar bill on the check. The boy rose behind him. "I'm goin' over," he said, "if you want a ride. I got a feelin' this is my lucky night."

"If you told me right I can guarantee it. Here's ten more—cover the odds board with buck bets and I'll cover line and field with the back up. You know the routine?"

"They'll beat our brains out if they catch us at it."

"Get smart. You don't even know me. I'll get there in about half an hour? Don't play nothin' but your own dough till then. You get a hundred or so ahead and you've made twenty. Just play the first roll comin' out, then take the opposite of my bet. We'll switch thirds."

"O.K."

"What time'll this game break up?"

"Three—-four ... who knows?"

"Just don't get greedy. It's twenty bucks on the hundred."

"That's fair enough."

"One more thing," Steve said. "When you come to work tomorrow, bring me a box of copper-jacket 38's."

CHAPTER NINE

The bellhop didn't even look up when Steve joined the game. There were six players around the table. One of them was the tall, curly-haired man the kid had described. He was playing the big six, wilting a few dollars until the dice came to him. When the dice passed to him, the kid spoke.

"Toss those money-makers, Curley—I gotta pay the rent." The bellboy put a chip on craps, seven, and eleven. Steve dropped a ten spot on the line and looked up at the man, pinning him with a grey stare.

"Seven, a natural. Pay the line and take them don't come," the bored stickman said. Steve raked the chip and let the bill lie. Not once did he take his eyes off the man. Curley let his fifty ride and the bellhop raked off the four to one he'd collected for his dollar.

"Natural earns a crap roll," Steve said, flipping the chip onto the crap square. The bellhop slid ten to the line. The dice jumped the string and came up like two staring eyes. Forty dollars in chips was shoved onto the craps square. "Rake 'em," said Steve, "and ten he don't come." The bellhop didn't play. Steve's eyes were still pinning the tall man. The dice pitched and bounced to the wall. They read four. The bellhop put a dollar on the hard-way and ten on the come line. The man rolled, and the dice read six and one.

Two hours later the bellhop had three hundred and forty dollars in front of him. Steve had one-eighty. Steve's eyes were still on the man at the far end of the table. Curley was rattled by the cold stare, and cursing colder dice.

"Cash me," he said, handing over his remaining chips. He had lost nearly two thousand.

"Me too," said Steve. "I think it's time for a drink."

The bellhop didn't look up. He was holding the dice now and dropped ten dollars on the line. He was tossing for a second pass when Steve followed the tall man out into the bar. Curley stood near the center of the bar, drinking rapidly. Steve passed by him to the end of the bar nearest the door. He ordered a double brandy and kept his stare on the man. He wondered whether this was the one Vicki had forced to drive to the edge of town, or if he were... the other one. He felt the push of the lump in his throat and his belly drew up into a tight little knot. He remembered with pain the idealized, worshipful picture he'd carried of Vicki... remembered how he had somehow always felt that she could do nothing wrong and he could do nothing right. It was a lost feeling... the same crippling helplessness within himself that goaded him and prodded him to exploit after empty exploit, and was never understood within him. To think of this man's hands on her... Steve's eyes sought the man again.

Uncomfortable under the stare, the man drank hurriedly and left. Steve followed him out into the dark night. The winter moon had set, and except for the patch of bloody snow under the neon sign, the street across the bridge to Omaha was dark. Steve turned in the opposite direction, toward the center of Council Bluffs. He had taken ten steps when he felt it, the press of a gun muzzle into the small of his back.

"Don't turn," the tall man said. "Just keep walking."

Steve walked, the man behind him. The gun no longer pressed his back, but he knew it was there, trained on him. "What is this..." he began.

"Shut up!" the voice snapped. "Turn in here, up this alley."

The alley was dark. Steve turned in. About ten steps further on, the command to stop came. Steve stopped. On command he placed his hands over his head and leaned forward until they rested against the building, supporting his weight. A hand patted down each side of his body. Satisfied that Steve carried no weapon, Curley allowed him to stand.

"Is this a heist?" Steve asked. "I ain't got nothin' much."

"I don't want money," the man said. "I want to know why you been givin' me the eye all night. Just what's your pitch?"

There are several things you can do when a man with a gun is asking questions. You can talk, you can gamble, or you can die. Steve decided to talk, and keep the gamble for a little later.

"I wanted a chance to talk to you," he said.

"So talk."

"Can I have a cigarette? It ain't easy to begin, and you scared me back there."

"Yeah, but don't play cute. I got an itch to burn you down. Don't make me do it...least not till I hear what you got to say." The tall man was amused by this, and his voice broke almost to a giggle at the end of his words.

Steve carefully and slowly reached into his suitcoat pocket, extracted cigarettes and an oversize book of matches. While his hands were in the pockets, he lifted the flap on the match folder and bent all of the matches down against the striking surface. He put a cigarette in his mouth. The man was a shadow in front of him in the pitch black alley, just beyond reach. Steve stripped out a single match and struck it toward the mass of those he had bent forward. Instantly he held a ball of flame in his hands. He pitched it straight into Curley's face. The gun roared, but Steve was no longer in front of it. Blinded by the sudden flash, Curley found Steve's hand on his gun arm and a lump of pain in his throat where the edge of Steve's right hand had bitten into his larynx like a blunt cleaver. A black pool of unconsciousness opened and Curley dove head-first into it.

Steve plunged his seared fingers into the snow to cool them, then applied the gun butt behind Curley's ear. He wanted him to stay unconsciousness for a while, at least. He picked up Curley, slipped, cursed, and then picked him up again. He had taken several steps toward the street when an idea crystallized in his mind. He dropped Curley and went through his pockets. If Vicki had lifted the car belonging to his partner, the idea would be no good. If this was the man whose car she had stolen, he would have some kind of a replacement.

Two sets of keys were in the man's coat pocket. One of the sets contained only two keys, and carried a tag for an auto rental agency. Steve dragged Curley deeper into the alley, then began looking for the car. The keys were for a General Motors unit, and only two of the seven cars that hung on into the wee hours in front of Marelli's were General Motors made. Steve calculated the chances of its being the Buick directly in front of the joint or the Chevrolet down the block. He walked past the Buick. It was a luxury automobile with all the extras. That left the Chevrolet coupe. The keys fit, and Steve forced the cold, protesting engine to haul itself back to the alley. He slid the man into the seat and then quickly drove out of town.

Eight miles out of Council Bluffs, he whipped the little Chevvie into the entrance of the Memorial forest he had seen from the truck the night before. Curley hadn't stirred, but wheezing rattles from his bruised throat told Steve that he hadn't killed him. The dry snow powdered into drifts along the park roadway. Steve stopped the car, opened the door, and toppled his inert passenger out into a particularly deep pile of snow. Slowly Curley came back to consciousness. When he could stand, rocking like a bubble in a Bendix, Steve helped him back into the car. The gun in Steve's hand was superfluous. For quite a while yet the man would have trouble enough just being in one place. Steve lashed the limp hands to the wheel with Curley's own muffler. Then he looked over the contents of the man's wallet. Folded down in the bill compartment was one item which was not explained … a piece of ticker tape. In the narrow shaft of light from the map light, Steve read it. It made no sense to him.

The tape was coded, and read: "XDR, Omaha, 217 W, up ... futures hold." Steve turned toward the tall man. The rattling wheeze in Curley's throat was easing now, and ..he found speech for the first time in thirty minutes. He began to curse, first at nothing, and then as he focused on what had happened to him, he began to direct the stream of invective at Steve. Steve laid the front sight of the pistol under the man's ear and pulled up, hard. "Shut up!" he snapped.

In the glove compartment of the car Steve found a pint bottle of whisky. He helped himself to a drink, then placed the bottle on the cowling of the dash. He turned his attention back to the man.

"Two days ago," he said, "you and some other crummy son-of-a-bitch proved what big men you were by kicking hell out of a woman in the Diegan Hotel. I want the other guy, Who is he?"

"I don't know what you're talking about."

The gun raked the ear again, faster and deeper. The flesh popped, then blood splattered against the man's neck. "Who is he?" Steve demanded.

"Eddie ... Eddie Rogers."

"Where is he?" Steve knew that Curley had cracked now. The name checked with the driver's license in the wallet Vicki had lifted.

"He's in the hospital. That broad fractured his skull when she hit him. She almost fractured mine."

Steve's heart jumped. If Vickie could be called for assault, or manslaughter ... "Is he gonna die?" he asked.

"No. They said he'd make it ... he ain't gonna die."

Steve felt the knot relax in his belly. "Who sent you after her?"

"Nobody." The man tried lying again. "We figured her for money."

"Talk sense. Nobody with money would live in that fleabag. Now knock it, small time. I want answers and I want 'em quick." Steve accented his last words by raking the back of the man's neck with the gunsight.

"Gimme a drink, will yuh?"

"Quite a lush, aren't you?" Steve helped himself to another drink, then spit the mouthful of liquor into the man's face. The alcohol spattered into his eyes like liquid fire. He screamed. "It'll get rougher, mister. Now talk.!"

"I don't know. Honest to God I don't. That tape, that's all I ever saw about her."

"All right, then. Read that tape back to me. It says 'XDR Omaha, 217 W, up ... futures hold.' What does it mean?"

"It means they want somebody, that's the X, in the Diegan for the D, the R means room and the numbers fit with it. The up means to work 'em over, and the two dots are the signature. The 'futures hold' on the end of the tape means you're supposed to hang onto the guy you work over until you get more orders." Beads of perspiration were standing out on the man's forehead.

"What does the W in there mean?"

"That you're after a woman."

Steve slapped the man with the gun, laying open the flesh along his jaw. It had been almost a reflex action when it happened. The man cringed. "That's the truth, honest it is!"

"Where'd you get this tape?"

"I pick up at any poolroom. The tape is right off the regular sports ticker. It wouldn't mean anything unless you got the code."

"Tell me about the code."

"It's a whole book, mostly names and addresses, but some other stuff like what you're supposed to do and how much you'll get paid."

"How do you get a code book?" Steve asked.

"It comes by mail. They change it every month or so. You never know when they're gonna change it."

"Where's your book?"

"In my room ... inside the band of a hat on the shelf."

"Who's the top man in Omaha?"

"I don't know. Don't hit me, I just don't know."

"How do you get paid off?"

"By mail."

"How do you let them know that you've got something, or that you did a job?"

"You just call the sports ticker service and tell them what to put on. You tell 'em that you're with the *Denver Gazette*."

"There isn't any *Denver Gazette*."

"All I know is that's what you tell the guy at the ticker office."

Steve thought about that one for a minute. It didn't make much sense. Almost everyone in the west knew that Denver had only the Post and the Rocky Mountain News. Still, a legitimate ticker service accepted code messages by phone for the *Denver Gazette*.

"What if you're reporting something that goes somewhere else besides Denver?" he said.

"It still goes to Denver first. It's all in the code book." "Now for the big one. How the hell did you know about the woman in 217? I don't want any crap about it, I want to know just how you knew."

"It came from Denver."

"But it had to go back to Denver from here when she was spotted. How in hell did they find out where she was, right down to the hotel room number?"

"I don't know. I'd tell you if I knew. I can't never go back now. They'll hunt me out, soon as they know that somebody else knows—and that you got the code from me."

"Who'll hunt you out?"

"That's what scares me. I...I don't even know. All I know is that a couple of guys have tried to lam out. Within a week or so we'd get a message over the ticker that put their code letter 'down six points.' It's hell, not knowin' where it's comin' from. That's why I jumped you tonight. I figured you were gonna burn me for lettin' the girl get away."

"Down six is the code for dead?"

"Yeah. It sure gives you a sick feelin' when you see them six little dots on that piece of tape."

"How do you guys know who's workin' with you?"

"We don't. There's three or four guys in a unit. I'm boss of my unit. I read the tape and use whoever I need."

"How much narcotics do you guys push?"

"Narcotics?" The man's face went blank. "I don't know nothin' about dope. All our jobs have been just to take care of guys."

Steve raked his neck with the gun again. "Narcotics, buster, don't care who handles 'em. Now, who the hell does if you don't?"

"I don't know. I can find a pusher if you want a fix. But I don't know who's the big man." The tall man cringed away in the seat, looking back at Steve. "All we ever handled was pickin' guys up. That's all."

With what he had been told of the syndicate operations, especially their recruiting and small-unit plans, Steve was willing to accept the explanation Curley had given. "I want that code book," Steve said. "Where do you live?"

Curley mumbled an address. Steve jotted it down. Most of what the man told him fit the pattern, but Steve still was a long way from knowing the story in Omaha. He slid out of the car, then went around to the driver's side, and pulled the door open. He grabbed the man's legs and pulled him out of the car. Curley's bound hands were still on the steering wheel. He hung there across the edge of the seat, his legs trailing in the snowy road.

"I've often wondered what kind of man could beat a woman in the belly. I think the son-of-a-bitch would be afraid of a belly beating himself."

Five minutes later Curley was a retching, sagging hulk, beyond further pain. Steve dumped him back into the car and drove as rapidly as the snow-covered road would permit. Steve spoke only once more as he pulled the car up to the curb of a lonely street in the Council Bluffs warehouse district.

"You got couple of hundred dollars; Curley. See how far you can run before you get down six." He sapped the man behind the other ear and rolled him out into the gutter.

CHAPTER TEN

Stopping at an all-night gasoline station, Steve found directions to the apartment house where Curley lived. He drove the few blocks, left the car, and let himself into the building with the second ring of keys he had taken from Curley. He checked the mailboxes, and a tiny key in the ring fit one of them. Inside was a letter with a Denver postmark and no return address. He stuffed it into his pocket and headed for the apartment bearing the same number as the mailbox.

No one was in the thick-carpeted hall. He let himself in, crossed and lowered the shades, and then turned on the lights. Quickly and efficiently he searched the place. The code book was in the hat on the shelf as Curley had told him. Except for clothing and empty whisky bottles, he found only three one-hundred dollar bills and a box of shells for Curley's .32 calibre belly-gun.

He left the apartment as the first streaks of dawn were showing in the east. Suddenly he felt very tired. A four-day binge, followed by an eight-hundred-mile truck ride would have been enough. These, coupled with the pace of the past twenty-four hours, left him exhausted. His blazing anger had cooled with the chance to act. His reaction to revenge was not elation. It was a release, and left behind it only exhaustion.

He drove the car into downtown Omaha. Just before he abandoned it on a side street two blocks from the decent hotel where he had first registered, he remembered the envelope he had taken from Curley's mailbox. He took it from his pocket and ripped it open. There was no message inserted, the envelope contained only money—sixty fifty-dollar bills. "The pay-off for taking Vicki," he thought. "Carazzi must have wanted her pretty bad."

From the time he had stood before the bar and pulled on his topcoat, he had worn the tight capeskin gloves. He checked the inside of the car carefully to insure that he had dropped nothing. He left the gutted envelope on the seat, the keys in the ignition. The remainder of the pint of whisky he slipped into his topcoat pocket along with the gun and shells. Then he opened the car door and walked away from it.

He entered the hotel and went to his room, too tired to care. He stepped inside the room, pulled the bottle from his pocket and drank two inches of the whisky. Like a tired fighter moving to his corner, he stepped out of his clothes and dropped into the bed.

It was mid-afternoon when a chambermaid tried his door and found it on the chain. He woke reluctantly, feeling the toll of the past week. A pulsating hangover steam-drilled his temples. Clumsily he hauled the phone from its cradle.

"Desk."

"Room Service." His mouth was full of cotton, and his voice grated in his ears.

"Service," a voice piped in his ear.

"How do I get six beers?"

"Sorry, sir, this is a dry state."

"Then send me up a messenger boy."

Ten dollars to the messenger with the promise of all the change if he made it back from Iowa in fifteen minutes was enough. Six bottles of black ale soon sat on the night table beside the bed. When two of them were empty, Steve began to feel alive again. He showered and shaved with the help of two more. Room service supplied a sirloin, three eggs over easy, and plenty of hot coffee. The glow faded with the coffee, but it took the hangover with it.

Steve pulled on his trousers when the bellboy brought them back from being pressed. He lay back across the bed and studied the eight-page code book until he knew he could translate messages. Then he left the hotel.

In a phone book he checked the address of the sports wire office in Omaha. If he was lucky, the volume of outgoing tape from Omaha would be light enough for him to find the strip concerning Vicki that had given Carazzi the go-ahead sign. He hailed a cab and crossed town to the tired building that housed the service. Sports ticker service had pretty well vanished with the upsurge of leased wire teletypes, but in the Midwest it was still used to settle baseball and football bets in the poolrooms.

The polish of the office had disappeared with the dwindling volume of business. An old operator with a bald head sat behind the desk, peering at his printer through steel-rimmed glasses and an old-fashioned green eyeshade. He looked as tired as his equipment. The old man held up one hand as Steve entered, finished his transmission, and then rose to saunter to the counter.

"Yessir," he said. "Where to and how many letters?"

"*Neon City News*, about sixty, I guess. I haven't scribed it yet."

"Take your time, young fella. The old tick doesn't run that hot. Not any more she don't."

Steve picked up a form and coded a hello message to his old friend John Rapp. He had no news, but labeled it in such a way that the operator wouldn't know he was just passing the time of day. He laid the message on the counter and the old man looked it over. He counted the words twice, summing the letters as he went. "Runs 73," he said. "Might as well take 80—don't cost no more."

"That's enough," Steve said. "How much?"

"Gotta charge you for all eighty letters. That's a dollar."

Steve flashed one of the bright new fifty-dollar bills he had taken from the envelope. "Smallest I got," he said.

"Thanks fer the compliment, son. I can't change no bill bigger'n' a ten. This place doesn't do fifty dollars walk-in business in six months. All our stuff is phoned in on regular accounts."

"How'd you like to keep the change?"

The old man's realization was slow. His rheumy eyes crawled up toward Steve's face suspiciously, the steel-rimmed glasses catching a spot of light and bouncing it at Steve's face. "You tryin' to pull somethin' crooked, young fella?"

"No." Steve tried a gamble on the old man. "About four or five days ago a message went out from Omaha slugged for the *Denver Gazette*. I want a copy."

"What fer?" the old man asked.

"A friend of mine got in trouble because of it. The sports desk there said he threw a basketball game. I know he didn't. I gotta prove it, that means I gotta find out who filed it from here."

"Was that the game at the University last Tuesday?"

"It wasn't a pitched game. I just want the guy who put out that rumor on my buddy."

The old man sighed. "That was my night off. I saw the game ... always have been crazy about basketball. CCNC lost to a better team—that wasn't no thrown game. Of course I ain't supposed to open up no record books here."

"How much tape you ground since then?"

"We don't send much more than fifty or a hundred feet a day. Our hot season is baseball time. The whole week's tape since last Sunday is in that wastebasket right there."

"Then I'll pay you just forty-nine bucks to let me be your janitor long enough to empty that basket."

"Sure couldn't get fired for cleanin' up the office, now, could I?" The old man chuckled. "Go ahead an' take it. I got a sack here I brought a couple of sandwiches in. Just use that to take it out."

Back in his room in the good hotel Steve poured over the yards of ticker tape. There were eleven messages slugged for the *Gazette*. Four of them concerned Vicki. The first translated out to, "Possible fill, your order. Pictures follow by mail." It was signed with the single letter "K." The second was apparently an answer to the direction tape Steve had taken from Curley, and said that

"X" had been taken. It was signed with Curley's code letter. Steve almost missed the third, it was so short. It read, "X lost 87-85," and could amount to sports copy if he had not had the code book.

The final message bore the time tag of 8:07 A.M. that day. It read, "Sub for X in 1 quarter, M, 61, BG, scored 18, Red, holds ball. UC transfer, C." Steve dug for the code book to translate it. Curley had filed one more message before he started running. When Steve finished working out the message he found it dealt with him. It said that Vicki was being helped by a man six feet one with black hair, grey eyes, weighing about 180 pounds, armed and in possession of a code book. The UC transfer meant 'use caution.'

He was described. Soon he would be known. Whatever he did in Omaha would have to be done fast. He picked up the phone and called the ticker service.

"Union Sports Service," the voice said.

"Pop, this is your new janitor. I know it isn't regulation, but I gotta have anything that comes from Denver, or came from Denver since eight this morning. How about it?"

"Can you come and get it?"

"No. Just read me the tape, will you? I'll have to have it, and quick. It's important."

"Hang on a minute."

Steve hung on for what seemed like an eternity. Then the old man was back on the, line. "There's one from Denver. Came in about 10 o'clock this morning. It just says, "X plus 1, DQRSDLMZ, UP Omaha, guarantee down ...... LQ ..."

"Count those dots to me, slow."

"After down they's one, two, three, four, five, six. Six of 'em there. Then after the LQ they's two. What's that mean?"

"They're gonna contest the libel suit," Steve said, dropping the phone back on the cradle. He sank back into the deep chair, looking at the code book. It was his death warrant. The message had gone to at least nine places in Omaha. The LQ was "locate immediately."

Steve felt a grinding in his belly. His palms soaped with sweat, and his mouth felt dry. He was hotter than a prostitute's dream and he knew it.

It took a moment or two for the full realization of the message to sink in—a few seconds for the objective fact to become subjective sensation and thus be understood. The past few hours of sleep and release were wiped out in the tiny row of dots that had fronted him with death. For that there was no narcotic of action or alcohol.

It had been a long time—nearly ten years—since Steve had been able to talk himself into a cavalier attitude toward imminent death. It was different now. The context had changed and the brutal beauty was squalid threat. It wouldn't be clean or what men rationalize as a purpose for dying. It wouldn't be like flashing out of the sky to a fantastic disintegration at the surface of the earth. No burst of flak over the pens at Wilhelmshaven or ripping Luftwaffe fighter matching him gun for gun now—now it would be dirty and ugly, with none to know why and profit from the knowing. The clean feeling of commitment he had known but a few hours before was gone. Instead of the clean and starkly magnificent course of tragedy, the script was cheap melodrama.

In a sense, though, there was no plea for exemption or escape. There could be no struggle and argument for an idea of being snatched from death by a squad of well-trained and fortunately timed marines. The inevitability of tragedy was still there, but colored by sensations accompanying the realization that tragedy is always a personal thing.

Steve sat, glue-mouthed and silent, for a long time. He tried to think, but the throb of the lump in his throat drowned the tiny noises his brain was trying to make. He reached for the pint bottle, trying to wash the lump out of his throat. He gagged the remaining whisky down too fast, and it bounced. He barely made it to the bathroom.

CHAPTER ELEVEN

Room service supplied Steve with a roll of adhesive tape. When the service boy had gone with his tip in hand, Steve rolled up his trouser leg and taped the long straight edge razor in the hollow of his calf. He checked the cylinder of the .32 he'd collected from the hoodlum the night before, slipped six more shells in the change plaque of his right hand coat pocket, and nested the gun in an inside coat pocket. Whatever kind of trouble might come, he felt a bit more ready for it.

Just before he left the room he counted the money he had intercepted. It totaled nearly $3,500, mostly in fifty-dollar bills. He sealed three thousand in one of the hotel envelopes, jacketed it with another envelope, and scribbled his father's address on it. Five stamps from his wallet guaranteed that it wouldn't be returned for lack of postage. He left the room then, dropping the letter into the brass mail chute by the elevators. "At least," he thought, "I've upped the ante on my insurance."

There were only two places left that Steve could find answers to the Omaha puzzle. The restaurant was one—the Diegan Hotel the other. There was no time left for subtleties. If anything were going to give, it would have to be right now. He left the lobby and walked east toward Council Bluffs. The restaurant was four blocks nearer than the Diegan. It would have to be first. He glanced at his watch. His timing was right. The watch read eight thirty. It was late enough to miss the evening meal crowd and too early for the after-show trade. The restaurant would be in a low trough of one of its periodic undulations.

The skinny counter man was leaning on his elbows, his stained chef's cap pushed back to expose a shiny pink scalp with straggly grey wisps of hair. The sports page of the local paper was between his elbows. Over near One of the booths the young, green waitress stood, vacuously leaning on her dreams. Steve entered and planted himself before the man.

"Yessir, what'll it be?"

"Coffee, black."

When the counterman came back with the heavy mug, the newspaper he had been reading was folded over Steve's hand. He put the coffee cup down and looked at Steve quizzically. "You want to look at the paper?" he inquired.

"I want to let you read some real sports copy," Steve said, "right off the ticker." He flipped him the piece of tape concerning Vicki. The man picked it up and looked at it. "Read it!" Steve snapped.

"It don't mean nothin' to me, mister. It's in code, ain't it?"

Steve lifted the corner of the newspaper. "Look what I've got in my hand and then read that tape to me!" he said. The man looked. Just a fraction of an inch of blued steel protruded from under the paper. "And I want it straight," Steve added.

The skinny man's eyes bugged. He looked at the tape again.

"XDR Omaha, 217M, up, futures hold," he squeaked.

"Who signed it?"

"It ain't signed. That's all there is, honest to God!"

"Don't let your voice get loud," Steve said quietly. "I want the answers to a lot of questions. Every answer you give me saves you from dyin'."

"O.K., anything. Take the money, anything."

"I'm no stick-up man. I told you I'm after information. About a week ago you hired a girl. Glasses, brown hair, good figure, maybe twenty-eight or nine."

"Yeah. That's right."

"She disappeared. When was that?"

"Four days ago. Never did come back to get her money for the three days she worked."

"Maybe she never will, unless you help me find her."

"You know more about her than I do. I only know that she came in the day I put the sign in the window. I gave her the job. She was good at it. She worked three day-shift tricks and then disappeared. I don't know any more, and that's the truth."

"I'll tell you, then. She got worked over by a gang of local boys. They nearly killed her. She got away from them and got to me. I want those boys. I want 'em bad. Now who did she talk to here?"

"Not me. And I don't think to anybody else, either. I own this joint, and my wife runs the day side. She said the girl never said anything except her name was Mabel Graves. Wife says the girl just wouldn't talk about nothin'."

Steve slipped the gun off the counter and dropped it into his coat pocket. "The girl is my wife," he said. "I didn't want to get rough, but I had to find out if you knew anything. That tape you read was what got her beaten up. If you had known what it meant, I'd have killed you. I'm gonna leave now. If you blow the whistle on me, they'll pick me up—maybe even put me away. I just want you to remember that they couldn't put me away forever and I'd be back to find you, personally."

The man took one look at the cold flame in Steve's eyes. "Mister," he said, "I didn't even see you. As a matter of fact, I hope you get just what you want. She seemed to be a nice kid."

Steve dropped a dime on the counter. "For the coffee," he said. He walked out of the diner and started for the Diegan.

The minute he entered the hotel he felt eyes on him. The usually vacant lobby had a pair of men entirely too engrossed in their newspapers. The fat desk clerk's empty eyes had taken on new tenants and no longer stared vacantly. The elevator boy stared a line down his back as he walked to the desk and picked up his key.

In the elevator, grinding upward toward the second floor, the silence cracked. "You're hot, buddy," the elevator boy said quietly.

"Those two in the lobby?"

"Yeah. They just came down from givin' your room a shake about a half-hour ago. They... they'll be back. I heard 'em goin' through your stuff."

The car was squeaking past the mezzanine. Steve reached over and pushed the stop button and the elevator jerked to a halt.

"How'd you make out in that crap game? You had three-eighty when I left."

"That's it. Here's yer dough." The kid handed over six fifty-dollar bills.

"Thanks, kid. I might not be able to collect later," Steve said. "But two of these fifties are yours if you'll tell me if the room across the hall is empty and open it for me."

The elevator boy passed over the metal-bound door key. "Two-fourteen," he said. "As a matter of fact there ain't nobody on the whole floor." He looked closely at Steve, and Steve handed him two fifty-dollar bills. The kid took them and slipped them into his pillbox hat. "Ready to go on up?" he asked.

Steve nodded, and the boy pushed the button again. When the car had ground the last eleven feet to the second floor, Steve slipped the door open carefully and looked out. The corridor was deserted. He fumbled in his pocket and took out the folded piece of tape he had shown the counterman. "Take this to that fat slob of a manager. We'll get lots of action then. But don't hurry... give me at least five minutes."

Steve practically ran down the hall to his room. He opened the door and retrieved his suitcase. He slipped back into the hall and opened the door of the room across the hall. He knew he had a moment to check his gear. He looked at the suitcase. It seemed to be in order, but the thread he had wound through the latch was broken. Everything was there, including the pistol. He checked the cylinder. It was full, and he slipped the cartridges out to check them. They were of the right weight. He closed the cylinder and thumbed the hammer back. He slipped his little finger into the groove. The firing pin was gone. He dropped the gun back into the suitcase and snapped it shut. In his pocket was the thirty-two caliber he had picked up from Curley the night before.

Outside, in the alley-like corridor, he heard the sound of men trying to move quietly. He dropped onto his belly and looked through the wide gap of the hall door, space that a good hotel would not have tolerated. There were three sets of feet near the door of his room. He stood back up, waiting in the dark of the room across the hall, then he heard the rapping on the door of the room he had rented.

"Manager, Mr. Blair. May I see you a moment?"

Steve ripped the door open and blasted a shot from the .32 calibre into the floor. "Freeze!" The three men went rigid, keeping their backs to Steve. "In here, slow and easy!" he snapped.

With his free hand Steve snapped on the overhead light in Room 214. The three men came in slowly, like automatons with sticky buttons. They went deep into the room and Steve swung the door shut behind them. "Now get your hands high. Move across to that bed and he down across it on your bellies with your hands on the floor." The three men did as they were told, the old iron bed groaning under their combined weights.

"I want to talk to just one of you," Steve said, "and to make sure I don't have trouble with the other two I've got a sleeping pill." He chopped with the gun butt twice, and the two. hoodlums obligingly went to sleep. "Now for you, fat boy! Rip that phone cord out."

The manager struggled off the bed like a human mountain and gathered the phone cord in his pudgy hands. He pulled, and the cord ripped off the baseboard. He stood there, a frightened and benumbed hulk, waiting for instruction.

"Tie your feet together at the ankles, and make sure it's tight."

The man gruntingly sat back on the bed and bound his ankles.

"Now get up."

The fat man rose. Steve came behind him and drove his left into the man's whisky-ruined kidney. The great slob screamed, went off balance and fell forward onto the floor, trying to reach his throbbing back.

"I'll kill you!" he screamed.

"You're wrong, scum. Any killing to be done here, I'm gonna do." Steve accented his remarks with a sharp kick into the other kidney. He kicked again. The man retched. He lay there, whimpering... waiting for the pain, arid willing to pay any price to avoid it. Then words flowed to avoid the pain, and Steve knew the answer to the Omaha puzzle.

Basically the operation was simple. Any time a syndicate victim tried to escape west of the Mississippi, the word went out to the syndicate hotels, tourist courts where syndicate call girls catered to the hot-pillow trade, and to the teams of men whose job it was to watch the first-line places. The word consisted of as complete a description as was possible. If any spotter saw what he considered a possibility, he filed complete descriptions and film by mail. Photographs were taken with buttonhole cameras. The direction for action came from the requesting source. Vicki's brown hair hadn't disguised her beauty and her fugitive terror had made her conspicuous. It had been her very bad luck to choose a syndicate hotel, but Carazzi's men would have tracked her down anyway. Her registering at the Diegan had only saved them a few days.

Steve bent and ripped the lapel camera from the manager's coat. At least Denver wouldn't know what he looked like when he got there. He helped the fat manager the rest of the way out of conscious contact with the world, then searched the three men. Only the manager had had a camera, but the other two men wore Colt automatics which they had intended to use on him. Their wallets yielded fifteen hundred dollars of syndicate money. He left the three unconscious men bound and gagged across the bed, closed the door behind him, and walked down to ring for the elevator.

"What happened up there?" the boy asked. "I thought I heard a shot."

"No kidding? Maybe it was a bed-slat breakin' under a couple of high-school kids?"

CHAPTER TWELVE

Steve walked rapidly away from the Diegan Hotel. With luck he might have a four-hour head start, and he didn't want to lose that advantage. He returned to his better hotel, gathered up the other suitcase, and packed all of his clothing into it. He put the useless thirty-eight pistol and the thirty-two caliber into the old pebble grain glad-stone he had brought from Neon City, making sure that they were wiped clean of prints. Then he put on his gloves and wiped all the surfaces of the bag again. Five dollars to a bellboy and enough money to cover the fare bought him a ticket to Limon, Colorado, on the next Rocket, and saw the bag checked through. When the bellboy had returned from the station and given him the claim check and railroad ticket, he was ready to move.

He reclaimed his identity from the hotel safe as he checked out. In the taxi he restored his papers to his wallet and his pockets. He took the train ticket and the faked identification and tore them into small bits. The tiny scraps of paper fluttered out into the Omaha night. Fifteen blocks away from the hotel he dropped the cab. Within a block of walking he had hailed another taxi. Fifteen minutes later he was drinking coffee in a truck stop on the west edge of Omaha.

The third cup of coffee was growing cold and oily before him when a load pulling for Dodge City drew in. The name of Scott Traybert was a password anywhere west of Neon. The counterman set it up, and Steve's transportation was assured. While the truck was being gassed up, the driver wrapped himself around the free steak with which Steve bought his ride. Steve sat quietly, writing down all that he had learned about the Omaha situation and outlining his next moves. He sealed it into an envelope and left it at the counter -for Scotty. Here at the huge way station, messages and clearance notes were common. Scotty stopped here for a fuel cargo and a good meal on any run that took him through Omaha.

Most of the ten hours of grinding up highway that took them from Omaha to Dodge City was taken up with many and lurid reminiscences about women, pay-loads, and gross tonnage … mostly women. Mike rattled on about this girl and that broad incessantly. Steve put in "uh-huhs" in their proper places, bought the coffee on their three stops, and simply wished that he could go to sleep.

His mind raced over the events of the last three days—calculating his chances of success in Denver! Only one thing was certain—the runner word would be out on him. He felt reasonably sure that his way out of Omaha would go undetected, but when no further leads turned up in Omaha, the search would broaden to all of the western cities.

"I remember a real broad in Peoria," Mike was admitting without pressure, "a hot little redheaded piece. What she had you never got before."

"What's that," Steve was thinking to himself, "leprosy?"

"… anyhow, she used to come down to the loading docks at Walker's and wait till I pulled in for a load. She'd have her car there, and we'd go up to her place while the boys was loadin' me out. Quite a joint it was, too."

Steve developed an interested tone. "Some of them are really fixed up," he said aloud.

"Boy, that's the livin' truth. She was built for loving and nothing else. Must have been one of them oversexed dames," Mike said with an air of authority.

Steve smiled to himself and thought of how undersexed many such women were—trying desperately to prove themselves to their own satisfaction. "I guess so, that's probably it."

When he could take the incessant recitation no longer, Steve told Mike he'd been on a long weekend with an Omaha woman and was just knocked out. This excuse Mike understood. After probing for details for about five minutes, he gave up and let Steve sleep.

The sun was high when the truck rolled into Dodge City. Steve shook himself awake and admonished Mike to "get a new set of glands before he got back to playin' those Peoria dames." Mike laid the truck into the curb and Steve swung down onto the street.

A bus put him in Lamar in the late afternoon. He called the ranch and his father drove in to pick him up. Rogers Ashe was a tall man, powerfully built and rawhide tough. His step was springy and his huge hands hung a good four inches from his lean thighs as he walked. His eyes, like those of his son, were steel-grey and penetrating. He was a man to reckon with, in any situation. He seized Steve's hand in a powerful grip.

"Good to have you home, son," he said.

"Good to be home, Pop."

The grey Plymouth had eaten up half of the eleven miles to the ranch when the next words were spoken. "That girl's in rough shape, Steve," the old man said. "What did you do about it?"

"I got one of the guys—she'd already taken care of the other one. She's tough, Pop, and here's something I never realized—she's got more guts than I ever imagined in a woman."

"You're still sold on her, aren't you?"

"Yes."

"What do you do now?"

"I go after the guy who ordered it done."

The old man laid the Plymouth off to the side of the road. "You mean," he asked, "somebody actually had that girl beaten up deliberately?"

"Yeah."

The old man's eyes burned a hole in Steve's face. "What kind of a low down cur could do that? And why?"

Steve laid it out for him, filling in all of the gaps that his phone conversation had left. It took about ten minutes to tell the whole story. When the telling was done, the old man turned his head to the open window and spat.

"How long will you be home for?" he asked.

"I'll leave for Denver in the morning," Steve replied.

Rogers Ashe pondered for a moment. "What'll we tell your mother?"

"What should we tell her?"

"I think we'd better tell her the whole story. It sure ain't pretty, but it'd be a lot easier to tell her why we're going."

"It's my job, Dad. I don't know anyone I'd rather have with me, but it's still my job."

The old man had seen that look on his son's face before. It showed itself more by a tightening of the jaw muscles and perhaps a slight narrowing of the eyes than by any really overt change. It was the same look that his face had taken on when Steve had tangled with some range-wild stallion in a battle for mastery. Determination, yes, but underneath a disquieting fear of himself that pushed Steve to be a lone wolf. Rogers Ashe swung his attention back to the road.

"Well, you can't do it here. Let's get on home and have some supper. We'll talk it out then."

The father slipped the little Plymouth in gear and ground out the remaining miles to the ranch. Both he and Steve were silent the rest of the trip.

CHAPTER THIRTEEN

It was sixty-four hours since Steve had left Vicki asleep in Scotty's truck. Now, across the table in his father's house, he saw her again. The bruises which the night had concealed were there, and the horror in her eyes was only beginning to soften under the realization that she was truly safe. He looked at her, trying to know how he felt about her.

He ate heavily, with a good show of delight in his mother's cooking…this was expected of him. The four of them sat there, with the roly-poly Juana clearing off the table and bringing in buckets of coffee and brick-sized chunks of deep-dish apple pie. Steve patted the Mexican's flabby backsides as she passed.

"Querida," he said, "tu tienes muchas carnes."

Martha Ashe looked up in horror. "Steven!" she said. "She can probably still wash your mouth out with soap."

The deep mahogany of Juana's face split its wrinkles in a toothy smile. Her eyes danced and from somewhere deep in the midst of her flesh the musical laugh of the mestiza emerged. Rogers Ashe sat back in his chair and roared.

Even Vicki's tired face lit up with the highlights of a smile which Steve remembered well. It was the look she had often flashed at him as she took him through some fascinating adventure in literature or music—modified now with the satisfaction given a creator in looking at the finished product.

Steve, in remembering, found himself thinking of the good-natured but unremitting punishment which Juana had ladled out to him in his youth. She was a fixture in the Ashe household, enjoying all of the rights and privileges which some ebony house-servant had known in his grandfather's house in Virginia. He glanced up and across the table at Vicki. Sadness and fear settled back on her face. Steve's chuckle died hard in his throat. He viciously attacked a slab of the cinnamon-darkened pie.

When the cups were refilled and the pie-plates removed, the real conversation began. Martha Ashe had known only the outlines of the story—that Vicki was in danger and was to be helped—but she had known nothing of the extent of the disaster which surrounded her. As she looked at Vicki now, it was more than a glance. It was a long appraising stare. Then she looked at her son, realizing what he wouldn't even admit to himself. The feeling Martha Ashe was experiencing was not new to her. It had been there before—this sinking feeling in the pit of her stomach. It was the weight of continuing fear, pressing at her entrails like some great lump. This time it wouldn't end with the raucous roar of a plane put down on the Lamar emergency strip with Steve announcing that his personal war was over. This time it could end with him walking in the door as if nothing had happened, or with a call from the local police that they had been notified.

"When are you leaving?" she asked.

"Tomorrow morning, I guess," Steve said slowly. He felt it too—the inadequacy of words, the vacuum of commitment that became the insides of those who could invest only their hopes, fears, and prayers.

It was Vicki who broke the strain of the moment: "I don't want you to go, Steve," she said quietly. "It'll be all right in a few days, and then I'm going to leave. It isn't right to ask the impossible of anyone—much less of you. This is the twentieth century. The days of the Vendetta are over. Nothing more will happen— I'll see to that by just going away. So far away that I may be able to find a wind to blow the stink out of my hair."

Martha Ashe raised one of her work-worn hands as if admonishing some schoolgirl to silence. "I guess you never really saw my boy," she said, "or else you don't know much about this kind of man. He'll do what he feels he has to do. And," she injected almost as an afterthought, "it isn't a woman's job to stop it. You couldn't anyhow. He's a stubborn fool, just like his father." Her eyes were misty, and she reached out with both hands, dropping one on Steve's wrist and the other on Vicki's.

"But it isn't … it isn't fair to him."

"Remember me?" Steve injected. "I'm on the hook, too. I've been described, maybe even identified by now. I haven't any choice now. I'm no story-book knight on a white charger. If nothing else, I've clobbered a couple of their boys and collected more than four thousand dollars of syndicate money. I've broken a link in their code chain. It isn't a question of Vendetta. Maybe it was, but it isn't now. Now it's a matter of survival."

Vicki began to cry, silently. Martha rose from her chair and walked around the table to her. She stood beside her chair and put her hands on Vicki's shoulders, pushing back and shaking the girl's head to an upright position.

"One thing you've got to learn," she said, "is that when a decision is made, you've got to live with it." She spoke softly, while the voice inside of her said mockingly that there wasn't anything else you could do.

CHAPTER FOURTEEN

L ater that evening, the stars were brilliant. Steve stood looking at them alone, leaning on the gate of the corral, absent-mindedly feeding a handful of clover to the great black stallion he had broken and gentled two years before. It was still the chill of late winter, but down on the valley the first sprigs of green were showing in the watered areas. He stooped and grasped another handful from the small patch that was sheltered from the cold by the watering trough. The horse nuzzled his arms until he passed it through the rails.

Steve had been standing there a long time, body at ease and mind racing. No clear plan existed for his attack on Denver. Anything that he tried would be a gamble. Seeing Vicki again had turned an air-jet into the forge of his anger, and he burned with white rage. Of ways to do it he was uncertain, but of one thing he was certain—Carazzi was his target, and was to be the focal point of attack. First and foremost he wanted the feel of Carazzi's face dissolving into a pulp under his fists.

He heard the sound beside him, the rustle of paper. He started, then turned. His father stood beside him, rolling a cigarette.

"Want a tailor?" Steve asked.

"No, thanks. They don't taste good." Rogers finished rolling his cigarette. Steve fumbled out one of his own from the pack in his shirt pocket. In the flare of the match the two men's eyes met, then there was darkness again.

"How do you figure to get him?" the old man asked.

"I don't know. I've been thinkin' about it, but I just don't know."

"Sure you don't want me to go along?"

"I'm sure I do, but I'm not going to pull you into this. Besides, if they should know or find out who I am, they'll be here and you'll have plenty on your hands as it is." Steve sickened at the thought of it.

They stood quietly until the old man had finished his cigarette. "I'm putting a credit authorization through for you. It'll be at the 'Beef,' where you can just check it out." He used the range name for the Denver Cattlemen's Bank. "You might need it."

Steve swallowed hard. "Thanks, Pop, but we can fight them with their own money for a while yet, anyhow." He dug into his pocket and extracted his wallet. "Besides the money I mailed to you last night, I got a fistful here. Light a match, will you?"

In the flare of the match he extracted nearly two thousand dollars from his wallet. "Back your authorization with this and the money you'll get in the mail. With this and a little luck, we'll never get beyond it."

"You figurin' to live off them?"

"That'll make them come to me."

"Yeah, but that's like livin' on a bull's-eye. Livin' on a bull's-eye has only one advantage—the rent's cheap."

"I don't aim to take any long leases."

"Nobody does."

The two men dropped their cigarette butts into the dust and ground them out almost in a single motion. The old man turned for the house.

"How you aimin' to go in to Denver?" he asked.

"I'll get Jake to fly me up in the morning."

The old man grunted, then turned toward the house again. "G'night, son," he said.

Steve turned back to the fence. The black nuzzled at his sleeve demandingly, rubbing the rope hackamore against his arm and pushing his satiny nose against Steve's hand. Steve stooped and pulled another handful of the clover. He stood for several minutes, feeding the black a sprig at a time and making the horse nuzzle for each successive handful. Steve lit another cigarette, dragging deeply on it and watching the deep pools of fire reflected in the horse's eyes.

"Steve." It was Vicki's voice, soft and with a new huskiness. He turned. She stood beside him, wrapped in Rogers Ashe's hide jacket. "I've got to talk to you," she said.

"Vic, you shouldn't be out here. It's cold, and you ought to be resting."

"I couldn't be getting more rest than I am getting. I've been sleeping practically since I got here."

"You need it."

"Your folks are wonderful people, Steve. I didn't think there were any more like them."

"There are a whole lot of 'em, Vicki … if you just know where to look."

"Not like them—not like you."

"You always used to believe there were," he said. "Remember how you used to quote things to me? You never had any doubts about the qualities of people."

"I used to think a lot of things. I didn't know just what a stinking place this whole world was. I know now."

"It isn't all jungle, honey. It's a confused world, and there's more than enough viciousness to go around. But there are some open spaces, where a man can breathe and think and feel things that are clean and …"

"… and put himself up like a clay pigeon because some worthless tramp gets herself beat up?"

He reached for her and pulled her close to him. "Don't ever say that again. You … you're honest and worth …" He was going to say 'everything,' but he didn't. "Everything that honesty is worth." His arms ached with the feel of her. A warm file was rasping at his throat and his heart was pounding. She stepped back from him, aware of it, as if for the first time.

"How long," she said, "have you ..."

"Been in love with you?" He completed the statement for her. "A long time, I guess. But I didn't realize it until tonight. Not how I loved you, anyhow. I'd always just ... well, I'd always just thought of you as something that I wished all women could be like."

"That's great!" She said it bitterly. "I'm just right ... so very right for you." Her laugh bit a piece out of him.

"People don't stop being what they are underneath. You've been hurt in all the ways you didn't know existed, but you're still you."

"Not any more, I'm not."

"Yes you are, just like I'm still me ... still the same person who smells like sweaty horses and castile soap."

"You've never forgiven me that, have you?"

"I thought about it after I got to know you, and always felt that sick feeling when I thought you still had me down as a range goat."

"I never thought of you that way ... not a range goat. You've always been more of a mustang—range smart and tough."

"So you took that maverick and trained him, taught him all the gaits and jumps and then pushed him out to the riding academies. Only what you didn't know was how he felt. You'd given him training, all right, but you didn't know that he'd only want one rider."

"How could I know? I watched you grow so ... so damned competent." Her voice had picked up something new. There was a warm huskiness there as well as regret.

"I tried to tell you, once. It was when we were in school. I ... I couldn't. It wasn't the time."

He sensed her moving in the dark. "Why didn't you tell me? Why didn't you make me see what was there for me?"

"I couldn't think that you wanted me. I was just sort of an…experiment you felt a little proud of. You just sort of liked me."

"And beside that, no mustang ever admitted he wasn't wild and tough and able to take anything, is that it?" Her voice dropped lower. "Did it ever occur to you that I wanted you to need me? Right from the beginning I kept telling myself that I didn't love you, but I knew I was lying."

She was standing beside him. He took her hands and pulled her to him. After a long moment of holding her close, he let his hand move to her throat and turned her chin to meet the kiss. "I do love you, Vic. I always have, ever since I've known you…"

She broke away from him. "You can't want me now. I won't let you."

"You haven't got much to say about that, angel."

Her bitter laugh scorched his face and took another bite from something inside of him. "That's me," she said, "an angel with a tarnished halo." She twisted away and ran back through the night toward the house.

Steve started after her…then stopped. After a moment he slid between the rails of the corral fence, seized the rope halter of the black horse and vaulted onto his back. With the impact the huge stallion took two strides, then soared over the end fence of the corral, his bare back clamped between Steve's knees, Steve's hands twisted into his mane.

An hour later, when both were spent by the wild run of forgetfulness, they returned to the barn lot.

CHAPTER FIFTEEN

Jake Morris and Steve had flown together many times since the days when they had skipped afternoon classes at Lamar High School to hang around the airport. Steve's request for a boost to Denver was nothing unusual—Jake didn't raise an eyebrow, he just walked -toward the hangar and hauled the doors open to the sun which was screeching up out of Kansas.

"If you want to go alone I can let you have the Culver till Friday. I'd have to have it back then for the weekend, got it booked. First time it's been booked for six months, or you could have it, period."

"Thanks, Jake, but this is a one-way ride. I don't know when I'll be gettin' back, and besides I'm kinda rusty," Steve said.

"I got a big picture of you bein' rusty." Jake broke into a grin that blended his freckles into a solid brown mass from his chin to his hairline. "Anyhow," he added, "if all you want is transportation we'll take the Stinson. I gotta get back fast, and she'll travel better."

The two men wheeled the gull-wing out of the hangar and Steve slipped in on the right side. Just as he was priming the engine Jake remembered that he would be leaving the airport unattended. He reached under the seat for a card that read: "Back in ten minutes." He kicked the engine over and let it warm, then slipped out of the plane and walked back to the operations shack. He hung the sign over the doorknob and returned to the plane. Steve had toyed with the throttle and mixture controls, listening for the purr to develop through the ragged protests of the rudely-awakened cylinders of the little Scarab. He ran the engine up and checked the magnetos.

Five minutes later they were airborne. Jake picked up his altitude and wheeled to the Denver heading. He dipped the plane low over an outlying house and changed pitch twice. The propeller growled like a stick going down a picket fence in the hands of a small boy.

"Had to tell the old lady I'm out for a trial," he grinned to Steve. "She'd probably worry if she tried to call and didn't get an answer."

Steve made no reply. Jake looked across at him, sitting there with his hands in his lap, then tapped his shoulder and lifted both of his own hands from the controls. Steve picked up the dual wheel like a kid grabbing an ice-cream cone on a hot day. He clawed for altitude and found the ship responsive. He had something of the feeling that had been with him on his bareback ride across the drylands the night before. He nosed down, picked up speed and hauled up level, snapping the plane through three quick rolls. He laid over on her side and popped a pair of vertical reversements. They were headed for Trinidad—he drove the wheel toward the instrument panel, diving for the arid wasteland. He leveled out some fifty feet above the earth and hauled the Stinson back until she stood on her tail and then dropped over into an Immelmann. He came out pointing Denver.

Jake looked at him narrowly. "Either you're half-drunk, which I doubt, or somebody's in for grief when you get to Denver," he said. "This old gal's got to last me a while, Steve. If you wanted acrobatics we could have taken the Stearman."

Steve winced as his thoughtlessness was brought home to him. "Sorry, Jake," he said, "I just wanted a chance to think." He throttled back to the 160 cruising speed and let the plane fly itself toward Denver. An hour later he put her down on one of the small airstrips surrounding the city as gently as if he had been landing on eggs. There had been no conversation, only Jake's smile.

"Want to grab some coffee before you go back?" Steve asked.

"Naw, I guess not." Jake looked at him closely. "You huntin' a new woman?" he asked.

"No."

"Then I pity some guy you're after," Jake replied. "You're wound up like you were headed for Piccadilly Lillie."

"Just got some business," Steve said. He wrestled his bag out from behind the seat buckets. "How about me gassin' you up before you go back?"

"Don't need it. This old gal runs on the fumes. I got her weaned."

Steve knew better than to insult Jake with an offer of money. He raised a hand in salute and slid out of the plane. Jake saluted back at the closing door, gunned the engine and taxied to the end of the strip to clear with operations.

In the coffee Shop of the airport Steve had a second breakfast as he waited for the taxi called from downtown. It wasn't quite ten o'clock. The cab arrived as he finished his second cup of coffee. He paid the check and left the coffee shop for the taxi, then settled down for the fifteen-minute ride downtown. Mentally he inventoried his pockets and his bag. He had slightly over 900 dollars in his wallet, a pair of fifty-dollar bills taped under the insoles of his shoes, and a pair of loaded thirty-eight automatics in the bag. He opened the bag as the driver was concentrating on the traffic and slipped one of them into his topcoat pocket.

He had decided to operate out of the quietest hotel in Denver, and the cabbie dropped him at the curb without opening the door for him. This error in judgment cost the driver the difference between a dollar tip and a quarter, but he never knew why. The next stop was at the desk, and he checked in. He made one more stop in the lobby—at the cigar counter. He looked over the racks of newspapers carefully. There was no *Denver Gazette*. A pneumatic blonde sidled up to him.

"Yes sir, may I help you?" she inquired listlessly.

"The *Denver Gazette*? Do you have it?"

"No sir. It's privately circulated to bars and restaurants...places like that. You might find a copy in the hotel barbershop."

"Thanks," Steve said. "I guess I could use a shave."

She looked at him insolently, leaning forward while the square-cut neckline of her dress broke away from her breasts like rolling surf. "I think you're right," she purred, "there's nothing like a good close shave."

"No," said Steve, pursing his lips in an inaudible whistle, "but there are things that are a hell of a lot more fun."

CHAPTER SIXTEEN

The copy of the *Gazette* in the hotel barbershop was three weeks old. It bore the tag of Volume I, number 3. The masthead located the office on a side street a few blocks from the hotel. It also stated that it was sports magazine "of and for Denverites, published irregularly." Steve looked it over. To the layman it would pass as a professional job, but to the trained newsman it was simply the wire-service reports and features, neither edited nor rewritten. As a publication, it stank. Under his breath Steve mumbled the address and the staff names over several times, until he was sure he wouldn't forget them.

When the barber dusted off the customer ahead of him, he climbed into the chair and settled into the warm blackness of a pile of steaming towels. The barber began his inevitable monologue. Steve thought of the 3,500-year-old squelch of Aristophanes—the man who, when asked how he wished to be shaved, replied, "In silence." However, the razor was good, and the touch was velvet, so Steve relaxed and let his concern fall to his first try at breaking through to Carazzi. Steve had all the assurance of a man walking on eggs about doing this, and no ideas. All he had to sustain his effort was hatred, and like all hatreds, this one was essentially unproductive.

The barber's monologue broke through his reverie. He had seen Steve concentrating on the sports magazine, and had immediately presumed that a tip lay in sports conversation.

"Everybody in Denver is looking for a good heavyweight," the man was saying when Steve snapped back from future possibilities. "Even Mario Carazzi. Can you imagine him wanting a fighter? With all his dough he ought to be able to buy the champ, but he says he wants a local boy to build."

"Did you say Carazzi?" Steve asked.

"Yeah. Mr. Big himself. He wants a fighter. He's been hanging around the gym nowadays, the one down on fourth street, looking 'em all over. He don't want nothin' but a heavy. Ain't it funny, a little guy like Carazzi wantin' a heavyweight? He wouldn't go no more than welter himself, and he probably never hit a man in his life, but he wants a fighter."

"It figures," Steve said, thinking how some men like to own power—physical as well as all the other varieties. Steve's mind rapidly indexed all of the fighters that he knew. Only two heavyweights came anywhere near Carazzi's picture. Without knowing Carazzi except through Vicki's description Steve automatically felt that only one kind of fighter would appeal to him—the man who could simultaneously punish and out-think all comers. Carazzi would go for a fighter who hit hard, moved fast, and had a brutal way of keeping an opponent on his feet until he was permanently damaged. When Carazzi's kind of fight was over, one man would be on the floor, finished for all time. Carazzi wouldn't want a clean fighter, he would want a dirty fighter who could look clean.

"Me," the barber was saying, "I could never understand what there is about heavyweights that'll drive a man nuts. A guy like Carazzi would give up the best light or welter in the business if he could own some stumble-bum who bounced the scales at more than one-eighty."

"Just seems like they like 'em big, I guess," Steve said. His mind was racing over the possibility of an entry to Carazzi that would be rapid and yet somewhat unsuspected. It had been a long time since Steve had pulled on a pair of boxing gloves professionally. Part of his college education had come from his fists—club fights around Denver, Cheyenne, Omaha—but it had been a long time ago. He'd stayed in fair shape, but professional fighting had been a long time ago. Much time and much whisky. He was well over thirty, and even his weekly rounds with the boys in the Neon City police gym couldn't keep the years and the drinks from taking part of him. "It'll be rough," he thought.

The forty-five minutes after he left the barber chair was spent in laying together a boxing rig. He found a sporting-goods store and bought some shop-worn trunks, a pair of high-topped leather and chamois boxing shoes, and the cups, straps, socks, and towels of the journeyman boxer. He stuffed them all into a little zipper bag, paid for the rig and returned to his hotel room. He dug in his suitcase for a soiled shirt, retied his tie, and wrinkled his lapels. Satisfied that he came closer to looking the part, he left for the gym.

He put in the first twenty minutes on the gym floor, working on a light punching bag. He thumped it methodically, letting his eyes wander over the place occasionally. His timing had held up, and he mentally thanked the police captain at Neon City who had worked with him. A pair of middleweights were getting in a few rounds in the heavily padded practice ring. He draped a towel around his neck and went over to watch. He looked at the spectators more than the fighters. There were no men who matched Vicki's description of Carazzi among the watchers. He jabbed his thumbs into the top of his trunks, then looked down, eyeing the roll of fat around his middle, wondering how many he could stop before one stopped him.

The boys milling in the ring were fairly good. Both had good leads, but the counterpuncher in the white trunks had a way of suckering his opponent into a high cross that allowed for plenty of belly-pounding before the man could recover himself.

"Who's the boy in white?" he asked one of the sober on-lookers standing beside him.

"That's Frankie Jarad," the man replied without looking up.

"Clever boy. Who owns him?"

"Carazzi—who else?"

"Who's Carazzi?"

The man looked up then, quizzically eyeing the stranger with the worn trunks and the questions. "You a stranger in town?" he inquired. "Carazzi is the owner of the *Gazette* —the guy who brought the fight game back to Denver." Then he had Steve pegged. "Hey," he said, "I seen you go. Ain't you a heavy that worked around here a few years back?"

"I had a few."

"Steve Cottrell, ain't you?"

"That's the name I worked under."

"Where you been pushin'?"

"I haven't. Just figured that I was tired of diggin' ditches," Steve said.

"You still got it?"

Steve looked up with a wry grin. "That's what I'm here to find out," he said, "I haven't worked for a hell of a while."

The man looked him over. "Let's find out," he said. "You want to go a couple?"

"It's my first day, but I'll go three or four. Got any heavies who'll spar a couple with me?"

"I think we got one your size." The balding man went across the room and said a few words to the sweat-shirt-wrapped manager of the gym. Steve saw him turn to look, then go over to a bruiser who was working on the heavy bag. The fighter stopped punching, and he turned to look also; peering out from under the scarred brows of a face that had been hit with everything but success. Steve recognized the type, a workman—not a craftsman.

When the middleweights had ground out their fourth round, the gym manager came over to Steve. "Want to earn your work-out fee?" he asked.

"I need it, if that's what you mean."

"We're huntin' a heavy. Let's see what you got besides fat."

"Against him?" Steve nodded toward the battered heavyweight.

"Martinelli. He'll do. A good left hand."

"I need a few rounds … about four, I guess."

"Got gear?"

"Could use a headgear—I like my ears the way they are. Make it size 7 or better, then I'll go."

The manager disappeared toward the office and returned a few minutes later with a headgear. Steve set the webs in the crown of sweat-soaked leather and tried it on. Its clamminess against his flesh brought back a familiar scared expectancy.

"How hungry are you, kid?"

"Pretty low," Steve replied.

"Make this for keeps. I put in a call. If you look good, you might have it made. Jerry here tells me he's seen you go a few years back, and you looked good. If you still look good, you might fit the bill for a big man around here. He's lookin' for a heavy. I called him, and he's comin' over."

"I ain't goin' in for the kill unless there's some dough on the line."

"Take this guy and take him quick, and I'll give you fifty. I want to be the guy who finds Carazzi a good heavy. If you lose, it'll be nothin'."

"How straight was that about this guy havin' a rough left hand?"

"Pretty straight … but he throws it from a cocked shoulder. You'll have plenty of time to move if you know that."

"Thanks."

"How old are you?"

Steve lied without batting an eyelash. "Twenty-seven," he said.

"How much behind you?"

"Thirty-four wins, one draw, and twenty-nine full scores."

"That sounds good. Any big men?"

"I drew against Munn and whipped Gianelli twice."

"That'll really help."

Steve decided on the soft-pedal. "It was a while ago—I've just been workin' out since '46."

The manager's sleepy face contracted into a scowl. "That was a long while back, mister. I hope you still got it."

"So do I," Steve said. He looked across the room at the man who was to be his opponent. The man was a little old, but the lack of fat and the roll of his walk showed him to be one of the few who stay in top shape all of the time to keep from getting murdered. He was no patsy, and Steve visualized the leather that would be thrown at him. It did nothing to quiet the butterflies in his stomach.

"When do we start?" Steve asked.

"As soon as Carazzi gets here. I'm takin' a chance, kid. If you're not as good as you look and sound, he'll be climbin' all over my frame for bringin' him out to see yuh."

"Tell him I'm out of shape," Steve said lightly. He started some light warm-up, then stopped. "Can I have a tape job?"

"Sure. You plannin' to hit that hard?"

"I need a job…need it bad."

The fighter across the room saw that Steve's hands were being taped. He squared his shoulders and looked the reporter over carefully. He noted the tiny roll of fat above Steve's trunks with evident satisfaction. His smile was not lost on Steve.

About ten minutes later, Carazzi arrived. He said nothing to anyone. With two huge bruisers beside him he simply walked down to ringside like an emperor of ancient Rome and took a chair. He turned and nodded to the manager of the arena—the games could commence. The manager took Steve's arm and indicated Carazzi with a jerk of his head. Steve grinned and walked to the ring, walking with his fear. He took the box containing the white rubber mouthpiece in his taped hands. Fumbling it out of the box he bit off the two corners, tried it for fit, then extracted it and bit off some more of the right side. He held his hands out while the heavy gloves were lashed on, then tried the laces with his teeth. The bell sounded.

This was it.

CHAPTER SEVENTEEN

The first minute was one of feeling out. Martinelli slipped a left. Steve picked it out of the air with a chopping motion of his right. Steve tried a long-range lead, and his opponent rolled with it. They sparred ineffectually, picking each other's leads out of the air. Martinelli threw a sudden right. It caught Steve on the shoulder and sent him off balance. The dark bruiser followed with a quick pair of left hands to the head. Steve's roll-off was slow, and the punches stung and his ears rang. He backpedaled quickly. Martinelli followed, thinking he had him on the run, but Steve's left hand caught him on the right eye with a snap. Martinelli slowed, surprised. Steve ripped a pair of hard lefts to the belly, followed by a right. The dark man waded in, tying him up and raking the glove-strings across Steve's triceps on the break. The welt they raised felt like the brand of a hot iron. Steve snapped the left again, feinted with the right, then let a left hook graze the man, with plenty of push on the heel. A cut opened in the scar tissue under Martinelli's right eye. The bell sounded.

Steve went back to his corner, breathing as deeply as he could. He took a long drag from the bottle, then turned to spit. Carazzi was on the other side of the ropes, looking at him as intently as a biologist would look at a new specimen under the microscope. Steve opened to take the mouthpiece again, and the bell sounded.

Steve planted himself in the middle of the ring, waiting for his opponent to come to him. Come he did, with a pair of very fast jabs to the headgear stuck on Steve's head. Steve countered with a hook and tried to tie his man up. Martinelli stepped inside and drilled his right hand into Steve's belly. It doubled him slightly. Steve saw the left shoulder drop into cock position. He ducked left and the hand sailed over his shoulder.

Quickly Steve took the opening, and drove his right hand into the man just below the breast-bone. He heard the loud grunt and ripped a left to the injured eye. The cotton-packed slit reopened and gushed blood. The man backed off, looking as surprised as two kids on a sofa when the family walks in. He sparred with Steve for a moment, then telegraphed the punch with the left Steve had been warned of—the shoulder dropped for the fast punch. Steve sidestepped the blow and rocked in a roundhouse right to the jaw. Martinelli, trapped in his own momentum, met the blow full on. It took him over the heart and his legs went rubbery. Steve crowded into the ropes, pinning his man against them. He held Martinelli up with short, pumping left jabs, and hammered his belly with the right. The man was pawing, trying to hang on.

Steve wanted the kill now. He came in on the man again, and a desperation right from out of nowhere caught him just below the belt. Steve's hands dropped like lead weights. He caught the retch in his throat and threw it back down to his protesting belly. His opponent was a telegrapher, but he was no pansy. The bell sounded.

Steve's thoughts were not of Carazzi now. Something more important had superseded. His only thought now was how to keep from being sick. The sixty seconds of rest pause were spent wrestling with his stomach, and the bell sounded again before the issue was decided.

He let Martinelli lead to him, then tied him up. He needed a few more seconds to clear out the lump of pain that his belly found too heavy to hold. The manager, acting referee, broke them up. Steve climbed on the bicycle and started back-pedaling. Martinelli pressed to get him toward the ropes. Steve got in another pair of left-hand shots to the injured eye. It was cut just below the headgear now, and began to flow, clouding the right eye. Steve began circling left, letting the curtain of blood help to shield him from the dark fighter.

One minute of the third round was gone when Steve brought his belly back under tenuous control. He put out a left to the bloody, swollen eye, twisting the punch to bring the maximum crimson gusher. The dark man countered with an overhand right that caught Steve's cheek and peeled flesh, from it. Steve circled left, pumping two fast right hands into the solar plexus. The ring-wise veteran turned with him. Steve saw the left shoulder drop again. He ducked right this time, and let the left hand whistle over his shoulder. With his own left he turned the chin of the off-balance fighter. Then his right hand pinned a sledge against the man's jaw. The dark man rocked, hands down and helpless. Steve dropped a pair of lefts into his belly like bricks into a pond, then chopped another right into the side of the man's head. Slowly, the man began the fall to the canvas. At the six count he rose to one knee. At eight he was on his feet, dazed. Steve came in on him again, showering a dozen rapid-fire lefts against the cut cheek, then driving a hard right to the side of the head. Martinelli reeled, helplessly. Steve stepped in and measured his man. He let the right go. The old fighter was no longer able to roll with it. It took him flush and clean on the chin. He pitched forward onto his face. Steve turned and walked back to his corner. When they fall that way, they don't get up.

The manager's eyes were shining as he came over to help with the gloves. "You still got it, kid," he said. "That was real purty."

Steve felt a little sick from a source other than the belly punches he had absorbed. The kind of fighting that kept a man on his feet until he was hurt inside turned his stomach. He'd won, but it wasn't the kind of a fight he'd be proud of, ever.

"I want to talk to you, kid."

Steve heard the voice behind his right shoulder. He turned and looked into the face of Mario Carazzi.

CHAPTER EIGHTEEN

Carazzi stood at ringside, one well-manicured hand resting on the ring apron. He looked up at Steve with the casual intentness of a cattle buyer assessing a Hereford. His eyes were black, like pits of primitive demand. His curly hair was slightly grey at the temples, highlighting the deep sub-surface color of his light olive skin. He broke an animated smile. In spite of his hatred Steve felt some of the magnetic appeal of the man. When Carazzi spoke, his voice had the mellowness of a fine Madeira.

"That was no accident?" he asked, nodding toward the opposite corner where the seconds were bringing the dark man up from some remote chamber of unconsciousness.

Steve hauled himself off the stool, his hands free of the gloves and wrappings. He pulled the towel across the back of his neck. Not once did his eyes leave Carazzi's face.

"If you had thought so, you wouldn't have asked," he said quietly.

Carazzi's gaze narrowed. Steve said no more. He parted the ropes and stepped out onto the ring apron, narrowly missing dropping his 190 pounds on Carazzi's hand. The hand moved. Steve walked down the steps. The two men stood facing each other at floor level. They were a contrast in all departments. In size, Steve held a forty-pound, five-inch advantage but could not overshadow the little man. Carazzi was lean, hard. Every line of his body was architecturally and functionally "right." He was relaxed, cat-like, without waste motion.

"When can we talk?" Carazzi asked.

Steve shrugged. "Right now I'm going to shower and get rubbed down. Then I want a steak. After that, any time will do."

"Get your steak at a place called Gearing's," Carazzi said. "It's across from the dog-track."

"So what do I do, fly there?"

"Marty will wait and bring you when you're ready," said Carazzi, nodding toward the man in the chalk-striped suit who had been sitting on his right during the bout.

"All right."

Carazzi spun on his heel and walked to the door. Steve watched him cross the floor, then started for the showers. His hammered midsection was giving him recurrent sharp twinges of pain laid over a continuous dull ache.

The balding gym manager closed up the space between them, spilling words out as he approached. "You got him, kid. Damnit, we got Carazzi—we got him!"

"Yeah?" Steve asked. "Are you sure it isn't the other way around?" He continued walking toward the shower room.

"Who's your manager? You got anybody?"

"I take my own cream, Jocko. All I want is a good trainer and a handful of good sparring partners."

"Wait a minute. I got you this break."

"Nuts! You wouldn't have cared if I'd gotten my head torn off. You stood to lose nothing. But you're out fifty bucks, and I'll take it now."

The manager took his arm to stop him. "I got somethin' comin' to me, too," he said.

"I told you I can read my own contracts. If you want to work my corner it will be as a trainer-handler ... if you can do the job. I'll take care of the business end of it." Steve shrugged his arm and left the manager's hand clutching a handful of very thin air.

Steve took a very long, very hot shower, letting the hot needles from the spray bulb lance into his bruised belly and drain off the pain. His scraped cheek was beginning to puff and burn. He leaned against the cold-water pipe that fed the shower, pressing the battered cheek against it with his full weight. The icy pipe contracted the blood vessels in the area and the bump began to recede.

After the shower he went to the rubbing room and put up with a half-hour of kneading and hammering on his muscles. Coarse salt, smooth oil, and eventual alcohol carried away more of the pain. Physical pain could subside, but the lump deep in Steve's entrails was another matter. It was a hard core of remembered fear. He heard his own voice calling, "Yellow!" He saw the body arching through the air, the water closing around it. It was back as vividly and as frighteningly as that day when he was fourteen. He had the same frozen feeling that he had known so many times since then. He forced his eyes open and drove his mind back to the present. The fat masseur was still kneading his body. When Steve began to feel at ease with the residual aching, he told the rubber he'd had enough and went back to the shower pit.

The dark, scarred ring-veteran was there, slowly soaping his body and savoring the feel of the water. For a moment the silence was awkward, then the bruiser broke it.

"I hear you're goin' to sign with Carazzi."

"Maybe. He wants to talk, anyhow."

"You'll sign. You got what he wants." The man said it bitterly. There was something in his voice that made Steve turn to look at him, hard.

"Maybe. I need a break...need it bad."

"With that pair of dukes of yours you kin make your own break...but I want to tell you somethin', kid. There ain't no reason to hold a man up so long when you could dump him without he got hurt."

"I didn't want it that way—but the rumble had it that Carazzi wanted a mauler. I'd have...I'm damned hungry." Steve had changed his thought in mid-sentence, but it went unnoticed. He stuck out his hand. "No hard feelings?" he asked.

"No hard feelin's. I just got a boxin' lesson, that's all."

"You gave me one, too. That right hand to the belly you toss is a real heller."

"I thought I had you, but I was so out of gas that I couldn't follow it up."

"You damn near hit my backbone with it."

"You're soft yet. Six weeks trainin' from now and I wouldn't get in the same ring with you if I had a ball-bat. I'm in shape and look what you done to me." The man gestured toward his cut eye.

Steve took the man's shoulders in his hands and turned him around. Then he soaped the big man's back. As he was lathering the broad expanse, he pulled an idea out of the hat. He might need a friend, and soon. If he could sound this one out he might have a wedge to get help later. "If I sign with Carazzi, would you want a job?" he asked.

"Sparrin'?"

"Yeah."

"Providin' that you ain't out to impress nobody. Yeah, I like to eat regular."

Steve extended his hand again. "My name's Cottrell," he said, "Steve Cottrell."

"Al Martinelli," the dark man said. He took Steve's hand.

"What's the pitch with this Carazzi guy?" Steve asked, "Hell, everybody treats him like he was the big muck. I come in for a light workout and right away I'm matched over my head with a pitch to look good and go places."

"The guy wants a heavy, is all." Martinelli turned Steve and soaped his back. "He's had all the local boys trying to drop a couple of us for more than a month now. Up till today we ain't been up against a thing but a few Iowa plow jockeys and some" one-punch lilies."

"So what makes him want a chopper? Hell, he could get a dozen good heavies any time."

"Who knows from a guy like that? When people like him want something tested, we test it. If it ain't the right thing, they wait till they find what is right. He looked over some good clean boys in Kansas City last week—the kind who drop their man as quick and clean as possible. He wouldn't even talk to them. I know. One of them was my kid brother."

"Vince Martinelli?"

"Yeah, that's my kid brother."

"That kid's on his way. You mean that this Carazzi is such a knucklehead that he wouldn't want Vince Martinelli?" Steve's voice was incredulous.

"That's right. Vince is as clean and hard a hitter as there is in the game. He can .be the champ with the right handlin'. I know that just as well as I know my own name. He's like you—or like you were at his age—brains and style. But he … he ain't like you when it comes to slaughter." The man's look was appraising and still a little bitter. It was the look of a man with the feel of sweat-soaked leather ripping into him who still vaguely remembers hearing about fair play and sportsmanship.

"You don't like this Carazzi even a little, do you?"

"When I was a kid in Youngstown, I had a pet bull snake. I thought he was great. Then he swallowed a couple of kittens that a guy at the mill had given my kid sister. I ripped him open and the little cats were layin' there in his belly, all crushed and twisted. I get the same feelin' that I had about that snake every time I look at Carazzi."

"Just who is he, anyhow?" Steve inquired.

"He owns the *Sports Gazette*. I guess he's loaded with dough. From the crowd he keeps around he'd have to be. He's got every-thing on the string from fighters to painters and musicians—good ones, bad ones, phonies and the real articles. He's got 'em all."

"He pays the freight?"

"Yeah. I guess you could say that he's a collector—only he collects people."

CHAPTER NINETEEN

The large man in the chalk-striped suit was in the dressing room reading a paper when Steve returned from his second excursion into the shower room. Marty looked up briefly from his afternoon sheet, nodded, then returned to his perusal of the financial page, checking up his holdings in Dick Tracy.

Steve pulled on his clothes, whistling tunelessly and wishing that he'd brought a clean shirt, or that he hadn't worn the soiled one. He tied the tie carefully, put on his suit and topcoat. The right-hand coat pocket still weighed heavy with the automatic, and he wondered if the man had searched his clothing. He'd left all but a few dollars of his money in the hotel room, but the guns would have been a giveaway if a search had been made. He had thought of that and taped the other automatic up under the bottom of the dresser in the hotel room, but this one was here. If his clothes had been searched, he'd had it. If they hadn't, he might be shaken down before he got to Carazzi. He couldn't take the chance—he had to get rid of the gun.

The bitter scowl on Marty's face showed that he had progressed to Orphan Annie. The paper was up in front of him and he sat cocked on a chair. Steve rolled his trunks, cup, and sox in a towel. With his body blocking the big man's view, he slipped the automatic into the bottom of the little zipper bag he'd used to bring his gear to the gym, then laid the towel-wrapped bundle in on top of it. He closed the bag and turned to Marty. "Guess that's all," he said. "Let's go."

The big man put the paper aside with the reluctance of a bride at midnight and rose to his feet. "About time," he said. "The boss don't like waiting."

Martinelli emerged from the shower room just in time to give Steve the chance he needed. "Al," Steve said, "would you take care of this bag till I get back? Ask old baldy to put it in the office for me."

"Sure, Steve."

Steve's hunch paid off. In the parking lot at Gearing's restaurant the shakedown came. Steve climbed out of the car and the big man dropped behind him. "I don't take no chances with the boss's health. This is a gun in your back, so just hold it a minute."

Steve stopped between a pair of parked automobiles and allowed the big man to pat down his sides and hips. When Marty was altogether satisfied that he had no weapon, he took his hand from his pocket and motioned Steve on.

"I didn't want to do that," he said, "but I gotta follow orders—and one of 'em is that nobody gets close to the boss without we know where he stands."

"O.K., O.K., so now you know," Steve said wearily. "Let's get on in."

Inside Gearing's Carazzi smiled at Steve from across the room. Business was light. Perhaps a dozen people were in a dining room that could have accommodated the crowd of a hot high-school -football game.

No sooner had Steve seated himself than a waiter was at his elbow. From the reaction of the staff to a glance from Carazzi it was evident that all things were rendered to Caesar—even the things that were God's. Steve ordered his steak—with a large green salad and Caesar dressing and an avocado with bleu cheese instead of a vegetable. He ordered with the careless air of a gourmet. Carazzi eyed him narrowly once more.

No conversation interrupted Steve's demolition of the meal. When he arrived at the coffee and cigarette stage of the game, Carazzi's appraising stare vanished and he leaned forward to talk.

"All right," Carazzi said, "who are you?"

"Steve Cottrell."

"That's not what I mean. Run it down for me. Where are you from, what do you do besides fight, where did you learn to fight, and why aren't you the champion?"

"I'm from a ranch down in the Arkansas Valley. I've tried to make my living as a writer, managed to live without starving by writing for newspapers, learned to fight in college—put myself through by club-fighting. I'm not the champ because I wanted to be a writer. Now I know that if it's to be made, it'll be made by fists. I hope I'm not too late. Anything else?"

"You look like the kind of boy I've wanted," Carazzi said. "Just how good do you think you are?"

"Good enough to go up," Steve said. "And I'm going to go up."

"I suppose you know I've been wanting to find a good heavyweight."

"Yeah. I suppose you know that it was no accident that I turned up in that particular gym today."

"Your name is Steve Ashe. You come from Lamar. This morning you checked in at the Brown Palace Hotel. You've got about a thousand dollars in cash in your hotel. You flew here in a private plane with a friend this morning ... his name is Morris. You had coffee, then came right on straight to the hotel. You bought boxing gear the first thing after you left it. You went to the University of Colorado, paid your tuition by fighting under the name of Steve Cottrell. You graduated ten years ago—that makes you about thirty-two, not five years younger like you said. You were in service as a pilot—won eleven decorations and knocked down fourteen planes. You've got a reputation for driving yourself. Since 1945, you've been a newspaper reporter, most recently of the *Neon City News*. You broke a big story and then quit cold."

"So what else do you want to know?" Steve looked at him with a penetrating stare. "Apparently you've got a system for finding out that would be better than anything I could tell you."

"I can tell you even more. You push yourself hard because you're scared."

Steve's eyes snapped up and he started to rise.

"Sit down. You aren't scared of people…you're afraid of yourself. Somewhere along the line you started feeling that you really didn't have it…probably when you were a kid. You been pushin' yourself ever since. You're a congenital volunteer."

"All right, so you're a psychoanalyst, too. But how do you have my pedigree?"

"It's simple. You made a reputation as a fighter around here when you were in college. Some people remember you. When you turned up all of a sudden, I checked with some friends. The name Steve Ashe turned up on a flight plan at the Arapahoe airport this morning, and they remember that you took a cab. The cab trip record showed the Brown Palace. In your luggage was a letter of credit to the Cattleman's Bank and a Neon City press card. A few phone calls filled it in from there…calls to Boulder, Lamar, and Neon."

"Mighty quick service you get."

"Yeah. I also know that you arrived in Lamar on a bus out of-Cleveland. You were, probably broke. Your father has a cattle spread down there, and he signed the letter of credit—so he's probably backing you."

Steve's gaze did not wander, but he drew an inward sigh of relief that a couple of bits of information had gone unrecorded. So far as Carazzi's record went, it was phenomenal. It was luck that the bus Steve had taken from Dodge City was an interstate unit that had come by way of Neon and Cleveland. The Omaha tie-up had not mixed itself into the package of data. Steve was also happy that he had taped the other automatic out of sight instead of leaving it in the bag in the hotel Under the dresser it would go unnoticed in most searches. Leaving the bag packed except for a couple of shirts spread on the bed was also a lucky accident. When the room had been shaken, there had been nothing to indicate that he was belligerent toward anyone.

"So what happens now?" he asked.

Carazzi looked up. "You want to see if you still can make the grade to the big-time. I want to see that, too. But, before we talk business, what's this name Cottrell?"

"I've got a mother—she doesn't want me to be a fighter—but I'm all done with starving on less than a hundred a week. My old man staked me, and I'm going up. Until I get somewhere, she won't know about it. By then we'll find some way to tell her."

"All right, kid. I want you. Now what do you want?"

"I'm fighting for myself. You want a champion, but you don't know what to do with more money. I need that money. If you want me, I've got a deal for you. I'll take 90 percent of the gross and pay my own handlers and sparring partners. You can handle promotion and publicity on ten percent. You'll get your boy going up."

"Martinelli must have hit you pretty hard."

"That's my deal."

"My deal is a split down the middle, 50 percent of the net to each of us."

"Checking me like you did, you know I won't haggle. Take the deal my way or else I've got to say the conversation and the lunch were pleasant—but no thanks."

"I never have an investment I can't make money on."

"So what have you invested? The fifty bucks or so you used up checking me out? Drop by the Palace later and I'll give it back to you." Steve rose as if to leave.

"You really ask for trouble, don't you?" Carazzi asked the question softly, almost rhetorically. "You could be dead before you got to the parking lot."

"For fifty bucks? I doubt it."

"Sit down."

Steve returned to his seat. Carazzi looked at him, a cold admiration in his glance. Steve matched him, gaze for gaze.

"Also," the tall man added, "there's another condition. Every match goes on a separate contract. Nobody owns me —nobody but me, that is."

"When do you want to start training?"

"I started today."

"All right," Carazzi said, "you've got a deal. At least until you get your brains beaten out."

Steve lit another cigarette and called for more coffee. He eased back into his chair. Across the room someone dropped a coin into the juke box. Carazzi looked up at the head-waiter. The sound was cut off so suddenly that it might as well have been stillborn, and an irate customer was given his money back with the explanation that the machine was out of order.

"What slop!" Carazzi exclaimed distastefully. "Why is it that people never seem to appreciate good music?"

"Some do—but there are damned few juke boxes featuring Bach and Brahms."

"To me, there are only four composers," Carazzi said, "Mozart, Wagner, Handel...."

"And Hindemith, I imagine."

"How did you know?" Carazzi's look was one of genuine surprise, and it used portions of his face that had been out of the game so long they had lost their deceptiveness.

"It isn't too difficult," Steve said. "Mozart for emotionless precision—the counterpoint; Wagner for the drive of naked egoism; Handel for the mastery of the complex; and Hindemith for the stark conflict—the dissonance of struggle."

"I guess that makes us even," Carazzi said.

"How's that?"

"You know as much about me as if you'd had me checked out."

CHAPTER TWENTY

Carazzi's apartment spilled over with people in a very discreet fashion. Conversation flowed, gay and sparkling, yet it was muted conversation—muted in deference to the coming of the regent. Here and there were little knots of people gathered about the leggy, Florida-tanned women that his court demanded. Others gathered about the less obviously stimulating of his entourage. A few watched the adept charcoal strokes of a sketching artist—several gathered around an improvising pianist—still more discussed the relative merits of the beverages at the well-stocked bar. Fighting and fighters made up another conversation piece, as did racing and horses. Medicine was represented at court in its fashionable aspects of neurosis and ulcer with perhaps a few discerning psychosomatic specialists. There were none of the plumbers of surgery or the reaming proctologists, or the swabbing, painting and dosing practitioners. Law was there—the sort of law that shows up in the tailored perfection of Brooks Brothers. Science was only vaguely represented, since chemistry and physics aligned only vaguely with an empire of the sort that Carazzi directed.

Steve stood alone at the end of the bar, a half-consumed glass of buttermilk before him. The fifteen days of physical torture and deprivation he had undergone since the first day he had met Carazzi had taken the bags from beneath his eyes and the fat from his middle. He was lean and hard as a greyhound, with every muscle of his body toned—tautened by his self-driving perfectionism. His muscles tingled with an urge to be thrown into action. Another week and he would be fully ready—the top of condition—but he couldn't wait that long. He was ready three weeks before the date he had set for Carazzi. He wanted it that way. If he was to succeed, it would have to be soon. He couldn't risk letting the situation drag on until someone from Omaha checked in and identified him as the man Carazzi had destined for death. This was the first of Carazzi's invitations he had accepted for that very reason, but he felt that getting information in a hurry would be worth the risk.

All that he had pieced together in the fifteen days and nights since he had arrived in Denver was the gross outline of the Carazzi empire. Its nerve center was the office of the *Sports Gazette*, and processes from that ganglionic mass lay across the back of the Rocky Mountains. It stretched from Canada to the below-border brothels of Juarez, from the Utah salt flats to the brewery dregs of St. Louis, a fifteen-hundred-mile swath cut out of the center of America.

To Steve, it was fantastic. It was conceivable-in the work-drugged, mill-ground East, where people had learned to ignore their neighbors for fear of hurt. It was unthinkable here, in a region where the one common bond of all people was knowledge of their dependence on one another. Here the tradition was to feed the hungry, water the stranger's thirst. This was the place where one man's destiny was all men's destiny—and here it had happened. It was beyond belief. It had happened in a way entirely foreign to the West ... not with the clash of armed bands, as it might have happened a few dozen years before. The West was being sacked with stealth, avarice, and a hypnoidal needle. Carazzi was no cattle baron, holding his empire blatantly and brazenly against all comers. His was a malignant, spreading cancer, that sucked at the vitals of The patient. While this was going on, the patient herself—skin clear and proud breasts of mountains thrust against the unyielding sky—was congratulating herself on her good health and begging to be raped by force. Force was something that she understood and found almost welcome.

Steve's reverie was interrupted by the thigh-to-thigh pressure of the girl in the silver lamé dress. His gaze as he turned toward her revealed much unused bar space that she could have used. "Novel introduction," he said. "I'm Steve Cottrell."

"I know." She held his eyes in a penetrating stare, almost forcing him to stare back. Her years were few by the calendar, but there was an age-old knowledge reflected in her slightly hard features. The molten slate of her eyes looked like pools of desire into which a man would unhesitatingly wade. "My name is Rea Hartley. Thanks for looking at my eyes first."

He let his gaze sweep over her, and his taut muscles felt the inexorable tug of tension. From the simplicity of her black hair to the silver slippers on her feet, there was no line out of place. The look of her started a grinding in his stomach, and his flanks ached with the sudden flare of desire.

"Short for Oread, I imagine," he said.

"Yes, how did you know?"

"She was a wood nymph, wasn't she?"

She threw back her head and laughed. It was a genuine laugh, not the amused giggle of a little girl playing at sex. Her teeth gleamed against her red lips, and her face came alight with a quick, suffused glow. From her face the mirth descended into her body—her unbound breasts leapt forward and her shoulders pulsated. The final tremor of the laugh crossed like a ripple across the flat belly and died gently at her hips.

"Now that I'm properly chastened," she said, "what happens next?"

"I ask who you are, in addition to a wood nymph with a name."

"Stranger in town?"

"Not exactly. It's just that I want all of the information I can get before I tell you that I am mad about you."

"Oh. Well, if that's all ... I'm a girl of immodest appetites who likes tall men without spare flesh on them. Also," she added, I'm intrigued by a man who will stand alone in the kind of a rat-race we have here and drink buttermilk."

"That's easily taken care of. I'm in training. Carazzi says I'm next heavyweight champ of the world."

"You agree?"

"I could be—barring accident."

"Umm. Show me your muscles," she purred.

"Not now, darling. I'm just coy enough to want soft lights and music." Steve smiled at her. "Or were you perhaps going to claim insulted honor to see me slap hell out of your escort?"

"No escort. I come to Carazzi's parties alone. He ... he likes it that way."

Steve winced. His expression did not change. This he could have given as the answer if he had thought about it. After knowing Vicki it would take something like Rea to fill up the hole in Carazzi's ego and make him feel like a man again. It would require a woman who would pull no punches and reserve nothing—a woman with sweat on her belly and flame in her eyes.

"And how do you like it?" he asked.

"Any damned way I can get it—but it's got to be top-drawer. I'm no hall-bedroom girl."

Steve calculated. Women got close to Carazzi in time. Vicki had come into some information—and a woman like Rea ... "All of this pleasant chit-chat is dandy, but where do I call you?" he asked.

"You don't, but I can find you. Mario's bloodhounds stick too close for you to risk finding me. Where are you?"

"Palace, four-o-seven."

"Since you're in training you undoubtedly don't get out much. How soundly do you sleep?"

"Like a rock, except at about three in the morning—extra especially this morning."

"You know, Golden Boy, that if Carazzi once gets it in for you you'll never play your violin again." Rea's glance mocked him, and the lights were bounding crazily from the surface of her eyes.

"Yeah. I've heard he plays rough—especially about women. So what else is new?" Steve's tone mocked her in return. If there was an advantage here, he wanted it. If she did not have an inside track to Carazzi's operations, he didn't want the risk of the kind of affair she was looking for.

Somewhere along the line something had to give. There had to be a way inside. Every wall has a top or chink somewhere, but Steve was sure he couldn't spend the time it would take to find the chink, and the top would be a well-patrolled death trap. The best hope he could muster was for someone to be trapped into opening the gate for him. Rea Hartley looked like a capable gate-swinger. He decided to make the play.

Her eyes sought his again. This time it was not to melt him down, but to show him the portrait of terror that the grey curtain had masked up to this time. "I'm dead serious, big man," she said. "You look good. I want you to stay looking that way. If Carazzi decides it, you go out the hard way and you'd be no good to anyone. He's taken care of others. For now, you stand pretty good with him—but don't let that fool you. He won't take anything ... not from you ... or from anyone."

"Where does that leave us?" Steve's tone was a question, an invitation, and an answer—all at the same time.

"Maybe it leaves us nowhere."

"But maybe it leaves us somewhere?" This time it was Only the question.

Rea Hartley was beginning to reply. Her mouth was open to form the Words when the lull fell in the conversational storm of the room. Carazzi had joined his guests. She managed only the single word before she left the bar to join the rapidly expanding knot of people around the emperor.

"Three," she said.

CHAPTER TWENTY ONE

Shortly after eleven, Steve left the party quietly. Carazzi had forgotten one thing about having such a party. Almost everyone from the *Gazette* was in attendance, and the office of the magazine would be almost empty. Before leaving the party Steve bad counted carefully, and found that five of the regulars from the staff were there. He didn't know exactly what he might find, but he did know that he'd never have a better chance to check the office.

He returned to his hotel directly, making a point of being seen and noticed by the desk clerk, night manager, elevator operator, and janitor as he went to his room. It was the usual time for him to. be turning in, and he made it seem that this was an entirely routine night.

In the room he quickly changed for action. The dinner jacket and boiled shirt were replaced by an old pair of slacks and a heavy sweater. He slipped on a leather jacket, dropped all of his identification on the bureau, and slid his feet into the soft gym shoes: When he left the room he carried only a celluloid strip from his identification folder, a penknife, key and cigarettes with a plain match book. The only other thing was the automatic. He retrieved it from its hiding place under the bureau and folded up the heavy tapes that had held it out of sight behind the skirt board.

Outside in the hall he Strode quickly down to the service closet. The celluloid strip from his billfold slipped into the crack of the door and the well-used spring log retreated into its carrier.

He entered quickly and closed the door behind him. For the two weeks he had lived there, he had noticed the dumbwaiter in the room which carried linens as the afternoon maid worked in the service room. He fumbled his way across to the shaft, orienting himself with a single match from the booklet. The carriage was at the fifth floor, and he knew that it might be in use, or at least that moving it might call attention to the shaft. He felt in the darkened shaft for the ropes. They fed into a single-reeve pulley under the center of the car. If he could hold both of them, the car wouldn't move.

He breathed a moment, then swung himself into the darkened shaft. Slowly, with his feet braced against one wall, he let himself down the seventy feet to the basement. It seemed an arm-aching eternity before he felt the dank concrete and accumulated dust of years at the bottom of the shaft. He listened intently. When he was satisfied that the basement laundry room was unoccupied, he lifted the sliding door to the dumbwaiter slowly.

He heaved himself out of the shallow pit and looked around. The night service light was burning. At the far side of the room was a door that led to the basement proper. The wall to his right contained a pair of double doors and a small window. From the doors a ramp for wheeling in baskets of linens dropped the four feet from alley level to the sloping linen-room floor. He walked up the ramp and stepped out onto a steam pipe along the wall under the small, high, window. It was one of the old style frames, with spring pins locking it in place. He dropped back onto the ramp and down to the floor again. Crossing to the check-in desk he found a number of pencil stubs and a roll of gummed labels. He returned to the window and raised it. He inserted pencil stubs into the pinholes in the casing, then covered these with gummed tape. He let the window down again, trying it up and down several times until he was satisfied that it would not lock. He slipped the knife with which he had trimmed the pencils back into his pocket and hauled himself into the well of the window.

He was outside the hotel now, in the alley behind the building. He waited, crouching, for a moment, looking over the concrete parapet until he was sure the alley was empty.

Then he vaulted into the alley and walked swiftly away.

Three blocks later he was in an alley again, this time beyond the building that housed the *Gazette*. He looked at his watch. It was ten minutes before midnight.

"Timing is just about right," he muttered to himself, "I hope, anyway." Steve had been a police reporter long enough to know that the shift change of police would be taking place—that squad crews from all over the city would be reporting back to their garages for a full load of fuel arid a new crew. It was a time of necessary lull in the activities of the police—when he would stand the least chance of being detected by a cruising squad car.

The building was three floors. Both upper stories were taken up with the offices of the *Gazette*, and a delicatessen and a hardware teamed up to occupy the ground-floor space. Steve walked up the alley past the place. It was quiet. Nearly a block away from the building the alley joined with one which let out onto the street in front of the building. He walked back, wishing there were a fire escape on the back of the building.

When he reached the corner of the building again, he did not hesitate. He stepped up onto the barred grating of the rear window of the hardware store, swung onto the heavy drain pipe and hauled himself up to the second-floor ledge. He eased his way along the narrow ledge and tried the windows. They were locked. He retreated to the drain casing and climbed toward the third-floor ledge. It was narrower, and slanted out and down. He tried a tentative step, still holding onto the pipe. His foot slipped, the gym shoes squealing and his body swung away from the corner. He clutched the pipe. His forehead was Wet with nervous perspiration, and for a moment his muscles felt a tremor. His hands against the drain were strangely cold and damp. There was only one way to go now, and that was to the roof. He hauled himself astride the coping, then slipped onto the white graveled roof. He crouched there for a moment and let the thin cold air of Denver night into his tortured lungs.

A few feet away was the skylight. He crossed to it. Dimly lit by the gas flames of the lead tanks was the composing and machine room of the *Gazette*. The skylight was steel-framed, with glass and mesh wire panes. He ripped out the putty with the pocket knife, tearing out the glazier's points around the center pane of the lower row. The blade squawked as he forced it past the edge of the glass and pried. The pane lifted. He laid it on the gravel behind. him and reached through the aperture, fumbling for the latch. A heavy steel rod lay along the edge of the casing. He pulled it, and heard the click of the dogs that secured the skylight as they snapped open. Gently he raised the hatch-like sill. He had noticed the steel rod to the skylight on one of his tours of the plant. It ran from the wall behind the linotypes up and across the ceiling to the skylight. Lying on his belly across the open sill, he checked it with the flare of a match. It looked strong enough to support his weight. He grasped the sill and lowered himself into the hole.

Hand over hand he inched himself along toward the wall. The rod bent slightly beneath his weight, and creaked against the old plaster of the ceiling. His fingers grew numb with the pressure of his weight, and the rough-milled rod cut into his hands. It seemed an endless time full of pain and effort before his toes swung into the wall and he grasped the cog wheel of the vertical rod that activated the skylight. He slid down the rod and gained the floor.

Carazzi had an office on the floor below. Some kind of record would be inevitable for a syndicate. Steve knew he had to reach that office. He touch-taught himself the wall down to the last pornographic verse as he eased toward the door to the stairs and the second floor.

A trickle of light seeped under the door. He tried the keyhole and the crack under the door itself. He could see nothing on the stairs, and there was no sound. He stood up and eased the door open. Quietly and quickly he slipped out the door and down the stairs to the open room of desks which served the "staff" of the *Gazette*. Around the room, like cribs in a brothel, were the walled-in, glass-fronted offices. At the rear of the room was the door leading to Carazzi's offices, banked by the teletypes and ticker.

A light burned in the last cubicle. Steve froze in the shadows of the room and cursed himself silently. No outfit like Carazzi's would leave a ticker unattended. There would be a man in the cubicle that housed the light—a monitor for the nerve system of the syndicate.

Steve eased the automatic out of his jacket pocket and began edging his way along the front of the glassed-in cubicles, praying that there was only one man in the lighted one. He slipped a cartridge from his pocket. It was now or never. He hurled the cartridge across the room.

Glass shattered from the front of the opposite cubicle, the sound splitting the quiet of the room like an earthquake. Marty burst from the door, a gun in his hand. He took three steps and stopped, dragged up short by Steve's arm around his throat. The automatic in Steve's hand ground into his back, and he froze.

"Don't turn," Steve growled, "or you're dead."

He released Marty's throat and eased the gun away from his back. Lining his palm with the heavy automatic, Steve slapped him behind the ear and he folded like a Jacob's ladder. Steve ripped out the phone cord and bound the man, lashing wrists under knees and binding his ankles together. When Marty was trussed up, Steve shoved him into the kneehole of a desk and then slid another desk over to make a box around the unconscious man. If Marty came to now, he'd never get a look at his assailant.

The door to Carazzi's office was locked, but the celluloid strip worked the latch back. Steve crossed to the window, dropped the

Venetian blinds, and pulled the heavy draperies closed. Then he turned on the overhead light. Systematically and without hurry he went through the desk and the three filing cabinets. Anything that looked like evidence he piled on the desk. From the bottom drawer of the desk he collected a metal strongbox which he pried open with his pocket knife. It contained nearly forty thousand dollars and several lists of names—the pay lists. From one of the filing cabinets he. had gained several folders of information in code.

Steve glanced at his watch. It was nearly two o'clock. He took a large envelope box from the top of the cabinet and piled all the material in it. He placed the money in a manila envelope and put it on top, pulling the lid of the box into place.

Just before leaving the office he swept the blotter from the top of the large mahogany desk and took out his knife. He scratched a signature in the top of the desk, the knife biting deep into the smooth-grained wood. Perhaps, if he could rattle them, he could get more of a break than any other way. He spilled the file contents about the room and dumped the desk drawers.

He slipped out of the office and down the front, stairs to the door of the building. The street outside looked deserted. He slid the bolt and stepped out into the street, the box under his arm.

Behind him, in the office he had left a shambles, the overhead light still beamed down on the desk top and the raw, somehow profane cut of its single word.

"Blair."

CHAPTER TWENTY TWO

The box under his arm, Steve walked boldly down the street. He reached the alley that served the Brown Palace Hotel and turned in. His watch showed two-fifteen as he dropped over the edge of the rain parapet into the window well. The service light was still on, the laundry room still deserted. He slid the window up and dropped into the room, then pulled the gummed tape and pencils from the lock slots of the window. He crossed to the dumbwaiter shaft and dropped the box into the shallow pit, then climbed into the shaft himself. The box, shoved over into the corner of the well, could remain undiscovered for months.

He started the long climb back to the fourth floor, his arms growing leaden with the strain. He had climbed perhaps half the distance when he heard the sound of one of the doors to the shaft being opened. He braced his shoulders and feet against opposite walls and let go of the ropes. He heard the creak of the car descending and felt the frictional heat of the rope against his thigh. Forty feet below was the bottom of the shaft. He was trapped.

He took the long chance. Wrapping his legs about the moving rope, he leaned back and let the leather jacket on his shoulders rub along the side of the shaft. The car began moving faster under the added impetus of his weight. He seized the opposing rope with his hands. The rough hemp bit into his palms, but the car slowed and hit the stops lightly at the bottom of the shaft, leaving enough cramped space for his body.

When he heard the night supply man close the door to the shaft above him, Steve pushed the heavy carriage back up the shaft and struggled to his feet. He stepped out into the basement and tugged the car back down to below the level of the basement aperture. There was a two-foot gap above the car roof and the top sill of the loading port. He wriggled through it and stood on the top of the car. He knew he had only the time it would take the night man to come down in the service elevator and enter the room to load the linens for the day service crew. He began his climb again, his arms aching more with the strain since he dared not stop to rest muscles shrieking silently as he fought his way up. He was dripping with sweat when he reached the fourth floor. He rolled himself over the sill and lay on the floor of the linen room, panting. His head ached and blood pounded in his temples. The cords of his neck felt like constricting steel bands.

He wanted nothing so much as to lie there, but through his pain he heard the squeak of the car rising. He closed the chute door and crossed to the door of the service closet. It was quiet in the hall and his watch gave him only fifteen minutes—there was no time for a slow check of the hallway. He opened the door and stepped out quickly, hurrying to his room.

In the bathroom he surveyed the damage to his hands quickly, then stripped and stepped into the shower. The hot water invited him, but he didn't linger. His hands were raw from the rope, but as the soap bit into them he found they were not blistered. He stepped, dripping, from the shower and rubbed himself down quickly. He squashed the clothing he had shed into a ball and wrapped it in the leather jacket, placing it on the floor of the shower pit.

Flushing the toilet several times he got icy water in the tank, then pulled off the porcelain top and plunged his swollen hands into the cold water. It stung like needles, but the redness and swelling went down. A small pat of lanolin from his hair-dressing jar was warmed in his hands and then rubbed in well. His fingers began to soften and relax.

He crossed into the bedroom and pulled on the pants of his pajamas, lighting the tiny lamp on his desk. After taping the gun back under the bureau he crossed to the bed, ripped the covers back and stretched out to relax. It was one minute to three.

He was on his third cigarette when the knock came lightly on his door. He crossed the room and opened it. Rea Hartley entered without a word and shrugged out of her coat. She had exchanged the silver lamé evening sheath for a black, scoop-necked street dress.

"Hello," Steve said, "I was beginning to think you weren't coming."

"Hello," she breathed. "It wasn't easy to get away."

She crossed the room to him and wrapped him in her arms. Her touch was like a living, searing flame. She pulled his head down and when her lips met his he found them hot and eager and searching. It was a long kiss, meant to arouse him—and it did.

Finally, she pulled her mouth away and dropped her arms. She was breathing more rapidly now and her eyes were dark, gleaming pools.

"Where's the soft music?" she asked, crossing over and sitting on the edge of the bed. "The muscles I can see."

"Somewhat on the sudden side, aren't you? Or don't you believe in preliminaries?"

"Not when I'm with a main-event boy. Especially at three o'clock in the morning. I know what I came for."

"You've got a point there."

"Two of them, if you look."

"Closely?"

"What do you think?" She rose, and made a pair of deft movements, at the waist and then at the back of her neck. A gentle wriggle put a pile of black jersey around her ankles. There was nothing else to fall. Her body was long and lovely and well-formed, the round, firm breasts proudly arched, her hips and thighs full and rich. She let him take his long, deliberate look at her, then, with a half-mocking smile she walked toward him.

It was five o'clock when she stirred languorously in his arms and murmured, "It's good to be with a man again. And you're one hell of a man. You like the wood nymph?"

"Umm," Steve answered, "but I thought I was the one who was supposed to have the muscles."

CHAPTER TWENTY THREE

They lay there, relaxed in the quick intimacy of a newly-shared bed. With tension drained away, Rea curled like a great cat, rippling the muscles of her body in an occasional sensual stretch.

Steve lit a pair of cigarettes from the package on the night table and passed one over to her. He stayed propped up on one elbow, admiring the symmetry of her long flanks and sculptured breasts. She began another stretch, coupling it with the exhalation of a long stream of smoke in a sound that was almost a purr.

"Tell me about Carazzi," Steve said.

Her stretch became a shudder. Her relaxed frame became a bundle of taut muscles. She flared at him.

"What do you want from me? For once, just one time, I thought I was getting away from even having to think of that son-of-a-bitch. Now you rake it all up again." She was sitting bolt upright now, her hands making fists against her taut lean thighs.

"He's that bad?" Steve asked.

"Oh, no. He isn't bad or mean, or crude. He just isn't. He's so emotionless something makes me want to scream. With him it's something automatic—like getting gasoline for his car or putting a ribbon into a typewriter. It's just something that has to be done occasionally. Technically, it's excellent. Carazzi prides himself on doing everything well. But once—just once—if he'd enjoy it … if he'd get passionate, or tremble a little, or even just look hungry …"

"But, he doesn't."

"No," she said, "he doesn't. I'm funny, I guess. I don't want to be some love machine to be used by appointment only. I like men to meet me on the animal level as well as any other level. With me, sex is a two-way street. At least it ought to be."

"And with me—but that isn't what I meant. I've…" Steve chose the words carefully, "… well, if I'm going to be under contract to him I want to know what I'm up against."

"You. mean you're not under contract now?" Her voice was incredulous.

"No. He wanted it, but I told him I was my own boss and that I'd play each fight on a separate contract."

Rea looked at him wonderingly. "And he took that?"

"He didn't have any choice. It was the only way that I'd play."

"Keep it that way. But you're going to have to deliver, Golden Boy."

"What happens if I don't?"

"You wouldn't like it."

"He wouldn't have me burned down, would he?"

"Carazzi doesn't kill unless there's no other way, or unless he's hurt—but if you don't fight for him and win, you'll be no good to anyone."

"How's that?"

"I thought you were smart. Carazzi handles narcotics and women. He especially loves to make addicts out of people who let him down."

"Narcotics pushers specialize in making addicts of anyone."

"Not like Carazzi," she shuddered again. "He forces it on people he wants out of the way. -Then when they're hooked so deep that they have to stay in line to protect their supply, he cuts that supply off and lets them squirm."

"The lousy bastard." Steve's tone was quiet, but hard and bitter. Rea looked up at him narrowly, struck by the strange intensity of his voice.

"You hate his guts, don't you?"

"Yes."

"Then why do you want him?"

"Fighting is the only way I have left to get anywhere. I've tried other things, including starving. I don't like starving. What's your excuse?"

"I haven't any. I'm just stuck." Rea's face was sad, her eyes took on a far-away look: "At first I guess it was the excitement of being close to the kingpin of an outfit like this that got me into it. Then, after I was in—there wasn't any way out. There isn't any way out. I'm stuck with him."

"So why are you here with me? And what do you mean, there's no way out?"

"I'm here because I had to prove to myself that I could fire a man again—I had to know it. But there isn't any way out. Women have tried to get away from Carazzi before. They either wind up dead or in some notch house taking all the tricks they can get to keep up their dope supply. When they get too old ..." She was breathing rapidly, as frightened as a colt in high brush. "It isn't going to happen to me," she said passionately. "I'll stick to him until he wants to break it off. Maybe he'll just pass me on to one of his boys and then I can get away. That's what I hope, anyhow."

"How do you know?"

"I don't know. That's what scares me."

"I mean, how do you know you couldn't get out?"

"A girl before me tried it.. Just tried to walk away without causing any trouble. He told me about it—threatened me with it as a warning. He squeezed her savings out of her, put her on the needle, then kicked her out. When she tried to get help from the law, he tried to have her killed. I don't know what happened—she ran and he's still hunting her."

"He took her money? You mean he robbed her?"

"No, nothing that crude for Carazzi. He found out her folks owed money and put the squeeze on them, knowing that she'd come through with the money. That's mild. You should hear him tell it. He finds out where your loyalties are—the people that matter to you, then uses it. He counts on the normal things that hold people together. He knows they'll react in just the way he wants them to."

"There's more?"

"Plenty more. He made a whore out of the girl's kid sister. Hooked her with dope and put her in a house to earn it. Beautiful girl, too. I saw her once. It was part of his treatment for me. He brought her to his office while I was there and tortured her. I get sick just thinking about it. She was overdue for a fix, and he had her begging for it. He made her strip off her clothes and take the janitor right there on the floor before he'd let her at a supply. That's when I knew I'd have to stick—that there was no way out for me till he got tired of me." Rea's voice went lower. "That kid wasn't any more than seventeen years old, and ..."

"What happened to her? Where is she now?" Steve's voice was demanding, but Rea was so wound up in her narrative that she didn't notice the intensity of his interest.

"All I know is that she isn't in Denver any more. She's in Salt Lake City, as a call girl. At least that's all he said—that he wouldn't put her in a crib until she couldn't make the big play anymore."

"Why doesn't somebody kill him?"

"I wish, Oh God, how I wish someone would. I can't. I know that. I've thought about doing it—even tried to figure out how—but I can't ..." Rea began to sob and buried her face in the pillow. In a moment she lifted her head again and stared at Steve, her face distorted and ugly with despair. "Is there any way out? Any way at all?"

"There's got to be," Steve said, "just got to be."

CHAPTER TWENTY FOUR

Carazzi's rage over the *Gazette* office was monumental. The news swept Denver like another of the chill March winds. It too was cold, but there was no clothing or shelter from this wind for the man called "Blair."

Steve was in the gymnasium, working out on the light bag, when Carazzi, Marty, and one of his other bruisers strode in. They shouldered through the handlers and sparring mates gathered to watch Steve's timing. Carazzi gestured and at once the four of them were alone. The rest of the crowd had sudden business elsewhere. Steve continued to work on the bag.

"I want to talk to you," Carazzi said.

Steve nodded and glanced up at the large wall clock. "O.K., just a minute."

Marty laid his hand on Steve's shoulder and spun him around. Steve lashed out with the right hand he had been ready to throw. The fist in the hard practice glove took Marty flush in the mouth. He went down with a surprised look, glassy eyed.

"Keep your hands off me, fat boy!" Steve was standing over him as he spit out the words. A gun quickly appeared in the other bruiser's hand. Carazzi gestured impatiently and e man sheepishly put the gun away.

"What's eating you, Steve?" Carazzi asked.

"My room was shaken down again this morning while I was having breakfast. I don't go for that. Now what do you want?"

The vehemence of Steve's attack caught Carazzi unaware. Steve followed it up while the little man was still off balance. "Who shook my room, and why?"

"I don't know."

"If you don't, it's the first thing that's happened around here that you didn't know. We'll pass that. What did you come down here to talk about?"

"Your first go. Are you ready?"

"A couple more weeks, like I told you before. Who you got in mind?"

"Erickson."

"We're starting kind of big, aren't we?"

"He'll draw. Can you take him?"

"Probably. I'm pulling into shape fast."

"I think we'll, start you in Omaha. That's a good town for a gate."

The word Omaha cut deep—hitting Steve low and hard, but he managed to keep his expression from changing. "What about K. C.?" he asked. "That's a better fight town than Omaha." He knew if he argued against the Omaha assignment on any other grounds or with any especial vigor, Carazzi might check him out further. If he did, the fact that Steve Ashe and Curt Blair were the same person would put him dead center on a bull's-eye.

Carazzi's answer was bland and without hesitation. "If you should get dumped in Kansas City, you wouldn't draw fighting Marciano. In Omaha it wouldn't be so bad."

"Yeah … I suppose so. But I'm not gonna be stopped."

"I know that. As a matter of fact a couple of my friends from Omaha are coming in day after tomorrow. You can go back with them and taper off your training there—get used to the altitude difference gradually." Carazzi was scanning Steve's face, looking for a slip—a change of expression—a gesture. Steve gave him the gesture, but it was not the one that Carazzi had been looking for. He merely shrugged his shoulders.

"O.K.," Steve said. "When do we sign the match?"

"Friday."

"Anything else you want to talk about?"

"Yeah. Where'd you go last night when you left the party?"

"Back to the Palace and to bed. Why?"

"Somebody with a good set of muscles broke into my office at the *Gazette* last night. I want him."

"You too?" Steve asked. "Oh, I get it. You think it might have been me—or rather you thought it might. If I know you, you checked me out and found out that I went straight home, then had my joint inspected this morning. So why all the palaver now?"

"Has anybody been talking to you about me? Or about my set-up or my business?"

"Nobody except the guys around here, and that's all fight talk—you know, about percentages, contracts, bookings—Stuff like that."

"Who was the woman who was with you last night?"

"You're crazy, I went home alone."

"Just checking." Carazzi's face relaxed. "The night clerk said that a woman came in and across the lobby to the stairs about three—someone he didn't know. Just thought it might click."

"Real trusting guy, aren't you? It doesn't work with me."

"It's a big hotel, but it was a chance."

"Chance, my naked rear! Do your boys check everything?"

"Only when there's trouble."

"What kind of trouble? Just what did they get in your office?"

"Money—nearly forty thousand ... and some other things."

"No wonder you're checking! Is that why you had my room shaken?"

"What makes you think I did?"

"A couple of weeks ago we agreed that we were not going to underrate each other's intelligence."

"All right. My boys shook it, but I had to be sure."

"Are you sure now?"

"Yeah, I'm sure. If you want the truth, your showing up here in Denver was too pat to believe, and you fit the description of a guy I want for another deal. So ... I had to make sure."

Inside, Steve was slowing the race of his heart and gradually untying the knots in his intestines. "When you decide to shake my room next time, let me know and I'll help the boys hunt. They always mess up my laundry and never put it back."

"Do you know a guy named Blair?" Carazzi fired the question for surprise impact. The knots came back into Steve's belly with a sickening snap.

"Blair?" he asked. "Can't say that I do." He pondered the question for a moment, as if searching his memory. "No. It just doesn't ring any bells with me. Why?"

"He's the guy who wrecked my office."

"You mean you know him?"

"I never saw him—but he's a guy that caused me trouble in Omaha. He's here in Denver now. A guy with more guts than sense—he even carved his name in my desk."

"That doesn't sound very smart."

"It isn't. He's cagey, all right—wants to see me make a mistake. But," Carazzi sneered, "he can't bulldoze me into a panic with cheap theatricals like signing his work. Three men from Omaha can identify him, and they'll be here tomorrow. I'll have him in a day or two, at the latest."

"If he's still in Denver. Maybe he took your money and skipped."

"Maybe—I don't think so. He wants me as bad as I want him."

"What's his angle? Money?"

"No, it's a personal grudge. I guess he thinks he's an avenging angel or something."

"Old score for you two, I guess—none of my business."

"That's right. If anyone tries to pump you about anything, let me know, will you?"

"Sure. You're my meal ticket."

Carazzi turned to leave, the two hoodlums with him. Marty was holding a handkerchief to his bloody mouth. He flipped a look of untempered hatred at Steve.

"By the way," Steve said to Carazzi, "I need some clothes. How about an advance? I could pick out something this afternoon, then be all ready to go back to Omaha in a couple of days in case they'd need some alterations."

Carazzi pulled out a long leather bill envelope and extracted eight hundred-dollar bills.

"Give 'em to Jake," Steve said. "I'm gonna spar a few before I get into anything with pockets in it."

Carazzi and the two men left. Steve aimed a vicious hook at the dangling light punching bag. It jumped like a deer and racketed against the platform. He strode toward the showers.

CHAPTER TWENTY FIVE

Carazzi's having a heavy bodyguard was a possibility that Steve had only vaguely considered. Now it was going to be a real problem to get to him. Steve was thinking of this as he ran through a hasty shower. He was also thinking that anything he did would have to be done quickly. Even without the confirmation of the Omaha contingent, Carazzi had all of the information that it took to make Steve a dead man. If he should run over the information he had gotten from Boulder again, finding a connection between Steve and the Marotti family would be almost automatic. The thought of this caused Steve to scrub more rapidly. Carazzi had suspected him, and if there were any loopholes in the story he had just told the little man, a recheck would be in order. Even without the check, the Omaha men would appear for a manhunt in a matter of hours.

He sawed the towel across his shoulders viciously, his flesh reddening with the friction. He knew he couldn't counterpunch and slug with the Carazzi organization. The only course of action left was hit and run, gambling on the inertia of the group to slow its reflexes enough for him to be able to get away with it.

"I'm about as safe as a community cup in a cholera epidemic," he mused to himself. "Guess it's about time to get a little vaccine."

He dressed quickly, extracting the automatic from the little canvas bag in his locker and slipping it into his coat pocket. He stopped momentarily at the gym office and picked up the money Carazzi had left for him, then swaggered out of the gym as if hurrying were the last thing on his mind.

Once outside he began to walk briskly. Three blocks away he stopped at a drugstore and bought several dollars' worth of telephone fodder. In the booth at the rear of the store he put in some calls. The first was to the ranch, and he brought his father up to date on the situation and the danger. He could almost see the worried pucker of the old man's brows as he sat at the roll-top desk in the long sun room of the ranch.

"At best I've got about one day," Steve said, "and if I haven't broken the situation by then, you'd better be prepared for trouble down there. That's the first place Carazzi will start looking for Vicki."

"You got any idea you'll miss?" Rogers Ashe asked.

"It's a possibility. Maybe you'd better find some spot where you could hide Vicki out."

"She's in good shape now, Steve. We could ride out to the old line shack and stay there till we hear from you."

"And leave Mom alone with nobody but Juana? That wouldn't be good."

"That's true. It wouldn't work that way."

"In the morning put her in the barn loft. Give her that little Mauser pistol I brought back. She knows how to handle a gun. I think that would be best all around, then you can be there to look after all of them."

"Just one thing, son."

"What's that?"

"Don't miss."

The connection was broken. There was nothing more to say. Steve dropped a dime in the slot and dialed the number of the truck terminal. Scotty was in the barracks, sleeping after the latest run from Neon. Steve had them rout him out. Briefly he filled the big man in on the details. Scotty agreed to meet him at his hotel in an hour.

Steve made four rapid calls after that. The police lieutenant to whom Vicki had wanted to talk, the federal prosecutor, and the editors of both the Post and Rocky Mountain News, received the calls. All agreed to meet Curtis Blair in the prosecutor's office to get information on a narcotics operation. The meeting was set for two hours later.

"One wouldn't be enough," Steve thought to himself. "Carazzi might have bought one of them. If he's got all four in his pocket, I'll resign from the human race—that is I'll resign if I get the chance," he thought grimly.

He swung out of the phone booth and moved rapidly toward the front of the store. He paused at the front counter and used a dime for stamps and envelope. He slipped one of Carazzi's one-hundred-dollar bills in the envelope, sealed it, and penciled Jimmy Mahon's name and address on it. As he left the store he dropped the envelope in a mailbox on the corner, then continued on to his hotel.

Once in the lobby Steve went down the stairs to the men's room. He took his time now, to make sure the basement was clear, then he ducked through the service door into the laundry room—it was empty.

He retrieved the box from the bottom of the dumbwaiter shaft and went back to the men's room. A dime in the pay slot let him into a private office where he could look over the material he had stolen from Carazzi.

Fifteen minutes filled out the picture of the syndicate's Denver operations. With the code book he had memorized he could translate enough of the records for anyone to build a case. He put all of the material back into the box, stepped on the corners of the box until they broke under his weight and compressed its four inches to a size that he could jam into his belt. He put it inside his trouser band and buttoned his suit coat around it. After he put his loose-fitting topcoat back on and closed it around the bundle, he headed upstairs to his room.

He turned the key in the door and entered. He had taken perhaps two steps when he felt the gun muzzle prod into his back. He froze and a hand patted down his sides and removed the gun from his topcoat pocket.

"Now turn, muscle-boy," a voice said.

Steve turned and looked into the battered face of Marty, the man he had clouted in the gymnasium an hour before. "Nobody hits me and gets away with it—Carazzi or no Carazzi. Get over there, in the room!" the man snapped, gesturing with the gun.

Steve moved toward the center of the room.

"Now take that coat off. You and I got a score to settle," Marty said.

Steve peeled off the coat. Under the suitcoat the bulge of the box in his waistband showed up like a seven-month's pregnancy.

"What you got under your coat?" the big man asked.

"Nothin'."

"Just take it off, slow and easy-like."

Steve reluctantly peeled off the suitcoat. "Carazzi isn't gonna like this, you droppin' me. He'll wind you up like a two-bit top."

Sneeringly the big man gestured toward the bed. "Put that stuff in your belt on the bed and move away from it." The big man waited until Steve was twelve or more feet away, then pulled the cover off the squashed box. The stack of crisp fifty dollar bills in the envelope on top of the pile told him what the material was. "Now this is real dandy," Marty said. "It ain't gonna be me that Carazzi'll wind up like a top. He'll pin a medal on me just for catchin' you up. These things mean you're the one that clubbed me last night, and cleaned out the office. That makes two I owe you, and brother, you're gonna be paid in full, right now."

The man dropped the box onto the bed and walked toward Steve. He held the gun at belly level and crossed slowly toward him. "Turn around, muscles," he said. "This I'm going to enjoy."

Steve turned slowly, and the man chopped viciously at the back of his neck with the gun. A red flare went off behind Steve's eyes. He dove across the room toward the bureau and tried to roll away from the kick. He didn't make it. The heavy foot drove into his midsection. He rolled closer to the bureau trying to protect his fade with his arms. Marty kicked him again, rolling him across the room like some pain-filled drum. He tried to rise and the man kicked again. Steve dropped back, his head hitting the floor just under the bureau. Through the red glare of pain he saw the white strips of tape that held the second automatic pistol against the bottom of the dresser. He put his hands over his face—the man kicked for them, driving them away. Steve's right hand was under the bureau. He jerked the automatic free, and just as the foot was descending to make a bloody mess of his face, he rolled away and fired.

Marty's foot was arrested in mid-air. He-clutched for his belly and fell backward, a surprised look on his face.

CHAPTER TWENTY SIX

Steve dragged himself to his feet. Marty was writhing in pain, clutching at his abdomen. The gun he had chopped across Steve's neck lay on the floor. Steve kicked it away and knelt beside him, loosening his belt and pulling his shirt and pants away from the hole the thirty-eight had torn in his right side. Blood gushed from the wound. Steve put his thumbs just above the wound and began to press. The flow subsided somewhat. Then he released the pressure and the sudden spurt told him it was arterial bleeding. He ran to the bathroom and got a pair of huck towels, folding them into large compresses. He jerked two belts from his extra trousers in the closet and returned to Marty, binding the two towels over the holes. Then he ripped off Marty's belt. The little ashtray from the night stand fitted the spot where Steve's thumbs had checked the flow. He girded the belt .around Marty's waist and began to pull it tighter and tighter. The man screamed in agony.

"Sorry, no anesthetic but this." Steve chopped a jolting right to his jaw, and Marty slumped into oblivion.

Just as Steve had the final notch in the belt pressing the ashtray over the arterial pressure point, there was a hurried knock at the door. Steve opened it and was relieved to see Scotty.

"My God, Steve—what happened?" Scotty asked.

"I had to blast him—but he'll live if he gets help right away." Steve crossed to the phone and yelled for the house doctor, an ambulance, and the law. Then he grabbed up the box and his coats. "Let's get out of here, Scotty." He knelt and quickly wiped the prints from the automatic, then put it beside the unconscious man. He slipped the little belly gun Marty had carried into his pocket. They left the door open and hurried down the hall. A number of people were beginning to gather in the corridor.

The door to the linen closet was open for the afternoon service crew. They ducked into it just as the elevator doors slid open and feet began slamming down the hall.

"Over here, Scotty, quick!" Steve hauled the ropes until the dumbwaiter carriage was just below the floor level. The two men stepped on top of the car. It began a whining acceleration downward under their combined weight. Steve hauled on the rough hemp rope that was reeved through the top pulley of the car, and the carriage slowed. At the basement they jumped out of the pit and were out the back door before the startled attendant could get a look at either of them.

They bolted to the end of the alley, then slowed to a brisk walk and entered onto Carson Avenue, a block away from the hotel entrance. Steve flagged a cab and they were inside as the police cars began cluttering the area in front of the Brown Palace. Steve called the address of the federal building to the driver. They would be nearly a half-hour early, but this might be an advantage.

During the cab ride, Steve filled Traybert in on the details of the information in the box. His head was pounding from the lacing he had taken, and his ribs were beginning to pulsate from the kicks.

"They may be waiting for me—or Blair—at the building," he said, "but I've got to get this stuff in there."

"Remember the old hidden-ball play?" Scotty asked. "How about me taking the box? You get out of the cab and walk in. I go around the block and in the back way about five minutes later."

"It might work. If they've been tipped I'm sure to be jumped. But if they can't find the stuff they can't prove anything, and the information will still go through." He handed the box over to Traybert, and then, almost as an afterthought he gave him the gun, too. "It wouldn't do for me to have this on me either."

"What's the room number?"

"Two-eleven. Don't turn any of this stuff over unless there are four men there who can identify themselves positively."

The cab was drawing up to the front of the federal office building when Scotty spoke. "See you there in about five minutes. For God's sake, be careful."

"If I'm not there, you know what to tell them."

"I'll tell them everything that you've told me."

"Make sure all four of them are there—If I don't make it one of them has talked out of turn. Tell them that too."

"Yeah."

"Good luck, big guy."

Scott grabbed his arm as he was reaching for the door handle. "Steve," he said, "if anything goes wrong, I'm going to Lamar and look out for your folks and Vicki."

Steve said nothing. He gripped Traybert's hand hard, then reached back for the door handle. He left the cab and started casually for the entrance. The granite steps seemed a mile long, but he forced himself to climb them one by one. He expected lead in the itching spot of his back. None came. He made it to the lobby and began to breathe more easily. Inside there were more stairs, marble this time. He climbed them hurriedly and found Room 211. The hall was deserted and few sounds pressed on his ears. From some office he could hear the clack of a typewriter. A toilet flushed. He strode on down the hall, hearing his heels clack on the terrazzo. The shudder of water in the pipes in the wall had made him conscious of his battered appearance.

In the washroom he sponged his bruised neck and washed his rope-grimed hands. He looked at his watch. One of the kicks he had tried to guard against had caught it squarely, shattering the crystal and denting the hands into half-moons of hair-like steel. He took the watch off and dropped it into his pocket.

He opened the door to the washroom cautiously and looked toward Room 211. Scotty was coming down the hall. Steve looked in the other direction. The afternoon sun lighted a corridor at right angles to the one Scotty was in. It also cast a shadow—the shadow of a man at the corner. When the shadow began to move, so did Steve. When the face and a gun hand appeared around the corner he was perhaps ten feet from the intersection of the two corridors. He ripped the broken watch from his coat pocket and flung it into the face. Startled for a moment, the man froze. But then his gun roared in the marble corridor, and the shot ricocheted from the floor with a whine. Scotty dove for the wall and Steve went for the gunman. Before the man could fire a shot Steve was on him, his shoulder driving low into the man's belly. The impact of the tackle drove the two of them across the narrow corridor and into the opposite wall. With the air rammed out of his body, the gunman slid to the floor like a wet sack of meal. The gun dropped from his fingers. Steve scooped it up, but a blaze of pyrotechnics behind his eyes caused him to drop it again. He was reaching for warm black unconsciousness when he dimly heard a body crash into the wall beside him.

When Steve made the long climb back to consciousness, he was lying on a brown leather couch. There were five men in the room, watching him. He sat up. Scott Traybert put his hands on Steve's shoulders and gently pushed him down.

"Easy does it, Steve," he said.

"Who hit me?"

"One of Carazzi's boys. You should have known that they wouldn't try this alone—with just one man."

"Who are these guys?"

The tall, spare man spoke then. "I'm Lieutenant Morrow. You called me. This is the prosecutor, and these two men are editors."

"Good. Sorry that I had to be out when you arrived." Steve smiled without much conviction. "How much of the story has Mr. Traybert told you?"

"Nothing really," the federal man said. "You've only been out a few minutes, and we had quite a little action in that time. The man you took, and especially the one your friend hit, needed an ambulance ... so there hasn't been much time for talk."

Steve sat up again. "There's not much time for talk, anyhow. There isn't much time for anything but action, and the talk can come later. I'll tell you what I know as quickly as I can, so you can take action. Even this will take too much time—but sit down. I'll tell you all I can."

The men found chairs and Steve dragged himself to his feet to begin the explanation. He fumbled through the box on the desk and handed the money and the materials to the prosecutor.

"My name is Steven Ashe. Originally I come from Lamar. About three weeks ago I quit a job in Neon City. I was a police reporter for the News there." He nodded to the editors, and saw a gleam of recognition in the eyes of Adams of the Post.

"My friend, Mr. Traybert, offered me a ride to Denver in his truck. We were traveling west on Highway 30 in western Iowa when we had a minor collision with a car out of control. We stopped. In the car we found a woman savagely beaten. She is a friend of mine, and you men know her as a musician. Her name is Vicki Marotti. She told me she had discovered her ..." Steve gagged over the word "... friend, Mario Carazzi, trafficked in narcotics and white-slaving. She attempted to leave him. He set out to ruin her. He extorted her savings, forced her sister into prostitution, and forcibly made narcotics users of both her and her sister. After eleven days of narcotic treatment, she was left for dead in an alley. She recovered herself, cut herself off from any source of drugs until she could get along without them. She attempted to contact Lieutenant Morrow. Two men stopped her. One of them is named Larry Kenner, and the other she knew only as 'Jack.' She managed to escape and she got to Omaha. She changed her appearance and work and felt that she was safe. She was located in exactly three days. Two men held her captive in the Diegan Hotel in Omaha, and beat her to a pulp. These two men were Carazzi's agents."

"Incredible!" the editor of the News began. Steve cut him off with a wave of the hand.

"Please!" he said. "We haven't time. She managed to escape when one man left the room and the other attempted to assault her. She stole their automobile and began to run. An hour and a half later she collided with the truck in which we were riding. We took her with us, and Scott delivered her to a safe place. I stopped in Omaha, and was lucky enough to contact members of the gang. I used the name Curtis Blair, the name I gave you over the phone. I learned about their communications system. It operates over the regular sports service ticker in a special code. You will find the code in this box, and be able to watch that in the future." Steve paused for a breath, and to let the impact of the words drive deeper into the men's startled ears.

"While I was in Omaha, I learned that the messages of the organization there were sent to the office of the *Denver Gazette* in what could pass for sports code. I came here to develop what I could in Denver. I found Carazzi in the market for a heavyweight fighter. While I was at the University in Boulder I managed to support myself by boxing professionally. I felt that if I could get to Carazzi in this way I might be able to get enough evidence to make a case against him. Fortunately, I was able to impress him sufficiently, and I resumed the name I fought under ..."

"Steve Cottrell," Adams broke in. "I knew I had seen you somewhere."

"That's right. I managed to get Mario Carazzi interested in me and was able to move without being suspected of being Curtis Blair. I was able to get this material. You will find forty thousand dollars in this box. This money represents the payroll for narcotics pushers in Denver and central Colorado. A list of code names and pick-up points, as well as the amount to be paid to each man is there, too. Evidence enough for action."

The tall police lieutenant moved, grabbing for a telephone. The prosecutor hit the intercommunications unit on his desk. Simultaneously the two men began barking orders, reading names and addresses from the list. They ordered immediate raids on the *Gazette*, the apartment Carazzi occupied, and all known users, pushers, and suppliers of narcotics.

When the first flurry had died down, Steve looked at them all again. "There's more," he said. "The organization is divided into small units—single cells who get both their orders and pay without knowing their boss. An organizer lines them up, then disappears. Later the teletype lists this man as dead. 'Down six' is the code phrase for it. The recruits are cut off from any knowledge or contact with the man behind them. Their money comes from Denver in plain envelopes by regular mail. All of their messages must be directed to the *Gazette*. When someone is running away, the description of that person is put on the ticker to all of the cells. If any member of any cell thinks he has a possible suspect, he takes pictures of that individual and mails them to the *Gazette* office. This is how they found Miss Marotti."

The editors were making frantic notes. The prosecutor and the lieutenant went back to the phones to inform other units. Steve gave Scotty the high sign, then he pulled an envelope from his pocket and scribbled on it for a moment. He dropped it on the floor. The four men were still intent upon their tasks of the moment when Steve and Scotty bolted out the door and were out of sight, running down the stairs.

"Hey!" the prosecutor yelled. "Wait!" He rose from behind his desk and ran toward the door, the other three men close behind him. Steve and Scotty were bursting out the main entrance of the building by the time the men reached the corridor. The prosecutor turned back into the room and saw the envelope on the center of the rug. He picked it up and read what Steve had scribbled on it just before he and Scott fled.

"Your grand jury won't meet for several weeks, and I still have a job to do in this matter. When the time comes for testimony, contact Rogers Ashe at Lamar. I'll be there in forty-eight hours."

"That crazy fool!" the prosecutor exploded. "He'll be dead before then!"

CHAPTER TWENTY SEVEN

Steve had an idea of one place the law wouldn't cover to find Carazzi. If the raids missed taking him, Steve wanted to be there. Coming out of the side door of the federal building at a run, the two men managed to hail a cab.

Steve spilled out the address of Rea Hartley's apartment. It was the same apartment that Vicki had occupied when she was with Carazzi—the one she had moved out of before the final blow-off. A twenty-dollar bill waved under the cab driver's nose broke his respect for stop streets and speed laws, and it was less than twelve minutes later when they were dropped on the sidewalk before a luxury apartment in the Heights. They kept moving fast. Jabbing at a handful of buttons in the foyer, they were up the stairs before the lock stopped buzzing on the entry door.

The mailbox chart had indicated that Rea Hartley occupied a second-floor apartment. They reached the door and Steve knocked hurriedly. Scott had his hand on the gun in his pocket and was standing to the side of the door when it opened.

"Steve!" Rea's voice was a mixture of surprise and shock. He grabbed her wrist and yanked her out into the hall. "What do you think you're doing?" she yelled.

"Is Carazzi in there?"

"No."

"Good. We're in time, Scotty." Steve led the girl back into the apartment with Scott following them. "Now listen," he told her, "there isn't any time. Carazzi will probably be here in a minute—a few minutes anyhow. He'll be on the run. The law's after him. You've got your out if you want it, but it's gonna take guts."

Her face went the color of green wood smoke as the color drained away, leaving only a pair of blazing spots at her high cheeks to mark a faded anger. "What do you mean?" she asked. "You mean the law is moving on Carazzi?"

"That's it. You got your break a lot quicker than you expected. He's through in this town. They managed to get real evidence. The law may have him by now, but if I know Carazzi, he'll be here. They won't get him that easy, and besides that, I want him."

"What do you want me to do?"

"I want you to let him in, just like always."

"He has his own key."

"Good! That's all the better. In that case go into the bedroom and hide…even better than that, get into the bathroom and get down inside your tub and stay there. There's likely gonna be some shooting. Is there any other way in here?"

"The back door, but he never uses it."

"Could he?"

"Not if the guard chain were on."

"It will be. Now get out of here. Don't show your face until I come for you—or until Scotty here tells you it's all right."

She moved out of the room quickly, her fear lending her something besides her languorous strut. Steve took his position behind the door, and Scott Traybert with the gun stationed himself across the large living room. It was not a long wait.

Steve stood there looking at Scotty. It was like the big man to put himself dead center on the target. Steve envied the automatic courage it took. It didn't seem possible that Scotty could ever be frozen with fear. He would act, when the time came, with complete dependability. But Steve was gripped by fear. The sickening lump was back in his belly, and he saw the whole ugly picture again, the picture that had driven him since Warnie Johnson's death. Warnie had been only eleven, fighting as only an eleven-year-old will fight for a place with the older gang. The gang had centered around Steve, and so it had been Steve who proposed the "test of manhood" to the younger boy. Steve remembered Warnie climbing to the top of the railroad trestle and looking down at the water. He remembered calling him yellow. Then the little boy dove clumsily, his body flashing through the air in the liquid hell of an afternoon sun. Steve stood by the bank below the trestle and waited for Warnie to come up. Then, frightened by the unnatural quiet, he had broken and run away. It was the same now, except that it was Carazzi and not a reservoir that could swallow up a life. This time he couldn't turn and run. This time he'd have to act. Steve felt sick and afraid, not knowing whether he could do what had to be done. He was about to ask Scotty to trade places with him when he heard footsteps in the hall.

A key turned in the lock, and the door swung open to admit two men. Carazzi came in first, wrestling his key out of the lock. Steve reached around the door and grabbed his wrist, whirling him into the room. The second man went for a gun, and Scotty blasted a warning shot into the plaster beside the door.

"Drop it!" Traybert snapped. "Come in and join the party."

Steve had wrapped Carazzi's arm behind his back and was holding him. The bodyguard entered slowly, dropping the gun he had pulled. Steve kicked the door shut, then checked Carazzi for a gun. He was not armed. Steve shoved him „ across the end of the room to the couch, then motioned his bodyguard over to him. He bent and picked up the gun that the muscle-man had dropped. He took it across the room to Scotty.

"Just make sure we don't get any interference from any-one, Scott," he said. "This is one job I'm really going to enjoy." Steve turned back to Carazzi. The little man's face was no longer immobile … it carried shock and some tinge of disbelief.

"What is this, Steve?" he began.

"You were wondering about Curt Blair," he said. "That's me." Steve slipped out of his coat. "You wondered why he wanted your hide. Before I kick your brains loose, I'm gonna tell you. When you went all out to wreck Vicki Marotti and her family, you missed one member. Not a blood member, but I might as well have been. I lived at the Marottis' for nearly four years while I was in college. They're clean and decent—the kind of people you have to smash because you don't understand their motives—only their predictability. You took something clean and fine and left the stink of your filthy scum all over it. You nearly wrecked a whole region that's deep with integrity. You hit below the belt, any time you can, you filthy flesh peddler."

Carazzi hadn't moved, only whitened under the tirade. Steve reached down and grabbed his tie, hauling him to his feet. Carazzi kicked for his groin. Steve rolled and took it on his hip. He hit him, then, driving his left into Carazzi's belly. The little man was lean and hard, and he swung back, his heavy ring laying flesh open on Steve cheek. Steve drove his right into Carazzi's throat and Carazzi dropped, gasping for air.

Steve stood over him. Terror was showing in Carazzi's stricken eyes. "You hit below the belt, like this." Steve swung his foot in the short arc that terminated at Carazzi's groin, forcing a scream up from the cracked throat. He bent and picked the little man up, holding him erect with his left hand while he chopped him across the face with his right.

"You wanted a killer for a fighter, Carazzi. You wanted somebody who would keep a man on his feet until he was broken inside. Now you're going to know just how that feels. You're gonna be broken inside." He drove his right fist deep into Carazzi's belly, low. The man doubled. He was straightened up with a jolting left. The right hand thundered into his side, ramming his breath from his body and spilling him over the heavy coffee table. Steve left him lying across it and hammered at his belly and ribs with shattering force, driving fists into Carazzi's body like pistons.

"For God's sake, Steve. Don't kill him! That's enough!" Scotty broke in. He snapped Steve back from the table by wrapping a huge arm around his friend's shoulders. Steve struggled to get at Carazzi again—then began to calm.

"See if you can bring him around, Scott," he panted. "Maybe we can get him to talk."

"Take these guns, then. I'll get some water out of the kitchen."

Steve took the guns. He stuck one over his trousers and under his belt, and held the other on the panicky youngster who hadn't moved from the end of the couch. The kid was frozen there, his toughness drained away. He looked as if he wanted nothing so much as to be sick. Steve crossed to a chair opposite the couch and sat down, his emotion spent in the frenzy of the beating. He too felt as if he wanted to be sick.

Scott Traybert returned in a moment with wet towels and a pitcher of water. He dumped it over Carazzi and began trying to bring him around. It took more than ten minutes before a human look came back into Carazzi's glazed eyes. Until that time they looked out on nothing but the shock of brutality.

"Before I kill you, Mario," Steve said, "I want information."

The little Sicilian shot a glance of fear, hatred, admiration and pain—so mixed that it was impossible to separate them. "No dice," he croaked through his cracked throat.

"You like living, now. I can keep you alive a good long while—so long that dying will be something you'd pray for if you had any god but power. You know that, don't you?"

Carazzi nodded.

"Then talk. I want to know where you get dope."

"I don't know."

Steve thumbed back the hammer of the gun and let a shot go. It creased Carazzi's foot, and blood welled out of the slash in the custom-made shoes. "Talk!"

"It comes to me from L.A., but I don't know from whom."

"How did you get into this?"

"The same way all of us got in. We were organized by a guy named Mark. He came around and pegged us four years ago. I was just a little fish then. A few weeks after he left here the tape said he got the down six."

"Who's your contact in L.A.?"

"I don't know."

Steve thumbed back the hammer again. "This one takes your knee out—talk."

Carazzi's face went grey. "I don't know. That's the truth. We use the tape, just like all the rest. The only difference is that we slug our stuff for the Western Sports Leader." His throat ground as he said the words and he went into a prolonged paroxysm of coughing. "Water … Can't I have a drink?"

"Step out to the kitchen and get some more water, will you Scott?"

Scott went back into the kitchen. He returned at the point of a gun. The man who was to pick up Carazzi had come in the back way.

"Drop that gun," the new entrant snapped, "or your buddy gets it."

"Drop yours, or your boss gets it," Steve countered.

Carazzi's head turned toward his new hope, then he swung his gaze back to Steve. "I'm gonna get up and out that door," he said. "If you kill me, your fat friend gets it—probably you too. It's a simple deal—I live and you two live."

"Have your boy let Scotty move away, or you're a dead man, Carazzi."

"You can deal or not—however you want it."

"All right. I'll deal. But Scotty moves over to me first."

"I have your word?"

"I won't fire unless your goon gets trigger-happy."

"You said that I knew what motivated people. I knew you wouldn't let your friend die. I would, but you won't. That's why your word is good enough." Carazzi turned his voice to the man with the gun. "Let him go," he said, "but keep him covered from there."

Carazzi struggled to his feet. The young kid who had come in with him was up like a shot, slipping his hands under his master's shoulders and half-dragging, half-carrying him to the kitchen door. They delayed there only a minute. Carazzi had one more thing to say.

"We'll be meeting again," he said, in a voice that was a simple promise—not a threat. "When we do, I'll kill you."

The slender gunman stayed in the door to cover them, and Carazzi and the kid went out the back door. A few moments later a car horn sounded, and the gunman backed to the rear door. He was gone in a slam of the door and a clatter of stairs.

Scotty turned to look at Steve. "Why didn't you blast him?" he asked.

"I ... should have checked that guard chain. I forgot."

"Me too. Anyhow ... thanks."

CHAPTER TWENTY EIGHT

Steve made a quick phone call to Lieutenant Morrow's office, informing him that Carazzi had fled the heights district in a car with at least two other men, then hung up without identifying himself. He crossed to the bedroom door and called to Rea that it was all right. She came quickly into the room.

"What happened?" she asked, "I heard a shot...then later, there was another one. Who got shot? Where's Carazzi?"

"We had to let him go. One of Carazzi's boys got in the back way and got the drop on us."

"Then why aren't you dead?"

Scotty broke in. "Steve had a gun on Carazzi. It was sort of a trade. Steve guaranteed not to kill Carazzi if his boy didn't kill me."

"You mean you just let him walk out?"

Scott snorted, "You mean get carried out. The way Steve worked that guy over he won't be walking for a long time. One of those shots you heard creased his foot, but I imagine that Steve broke every bone in his body. He'll be laid up for weeks even without the foot wound. Even if the law doesn't get him he's out of circulation for a long while. I'm sure of that."

"Then I'm, out of it? Really out of it?" she asked with the pleading eyes of a cocker spaniel.

"I guess so," Steve said. "Denver would be too hot for Carazzi for a long time. There's a full-scale clean-up going on—all the way from Salt Lake City to the Mississippi. All the local cops are in on it, as well as the federal boys."

Rea collapsed into a chair. She was crying softly, without sobs and without sadness. Now that she was no longer on the edge of the knife blade, she began to relax her defenses, and the weight of her unshed tears broke the barrier. Her face was flushed and her eyes were streaming tears of relief. Steve and Scott were moving toward the door.

"Where are you going?" she asked. Her voice was calm, almost too calm. It was as if her voice were no more a part of her than the eyes which streamed tears independent of the rest of her.

Steve crossed back to her and drew her to her feet. He held her for a moment. "We've still got things to do, pigeon. I'd suggest that you cry yourself out, then get absolutely stone-dead drunk and sleep it off."

"Will I see you again?"

"Very likely. When I've finished what I started, I'll probably be back." He pulled the gun from his trouser band. "If any of your neighbors heard those shots," he said, "tell 'em you were cleaning this and it went off."

"There's nobody on this floor in the daytime. Practically nobody in the whole building except the super—not on a week-day, anyhow."

"Just the same, you take it." He put the gun down on the table beside her. She clung to him for a moment. He reached behind his neck and disentangled her arms. "I'll be back, lover—sometime."

She stood there motionless as he and Scotty left. No further words were spoken. The two men went out the door, and down to the street. Neither of them spoke as they walked down the hill toward the boulevard where they might find a taxi.

"I've been trying to think, Scotty. If you were racked up like Carazzi, where would you go to hide?"

"Good Lord! There are a million holes he could crawl into, Steve. He must have thought of something like this—must have some regular escape plan for just such a time. He sure wouldn't leave it to chance, not Carazzi. One thing is sure—it would be fairly close. He wouldn't risk trying to travel very far. Not with the kind of a line-up on a case like this. He'd hole up quick. They'll have to have a doctor —I suppose that it would be the same one who takes care of the boys who get careless."

Steve mused over these words for a moment as the two continued walking. "Well, maybe," he said, "maybe I've got an idea. Try it on for size and see if it could fit. Like you say, the hole would have to be someplace they could reach in an hour or so. It would have to be someplace they could get to without using main roads. It would have to be someplace where they could stay weeks without being seen. Maybe it's even in Denver."

"What about someplace that would operate only in certain times of the year? Like a country club in winter or a ski-lodge in summer?" Scotty asked.

"Sounds reasonable—but what if they get out by air?"

"Then there's no difference. If they get out by air they could be anywhere at all, so we couldn't worry about 'em."

"I don't really think they could get out by air. Not yet anyhow. Carazzi'll lay up for a while until he has time to get on his feet again."

"If he ever does get on his feet again."

"He will. I know that. He'll be out for our blood in a month."

"You goin' to try and find him before he finds you?"

"I'm gonna try for just a day or two. I've still got to find Gina and get her out of it before the roof caves in on her."

"Where do you start lookin' for a seventeen-year-old kid who could be anywhere?"

"The only lead I have is that she's a call-girl in Salt Lake City. I think it's pretty accurate. There's no choice. It's the only lead I've got." Steve slowed his walk, and turned his back to the wind to light a cigarette. "Want one?" he asked.

"Not now, thanks."

"I give Carazzi a month or so to get to the point where he can breathe against those ribs and walk on that foot. Maybe it won't even be that long. Then he's going to hit at us in every way possible. It will be a real Vendetta. It'll be a personal thing. Nobody else will be involved; even if Carazzi had an army, he'd come alone. That gives me at most about three weeks to find Gina and get her out of whatever she's in. I'll have to be back at the ranch before Carazzi gets there. He'll start looking for me there—or for anybody who represents me—so I've got to be there."

"How do you figure to find him before you go to Salt Lake?" Scott asked as they continued to walk down the boulevard, looking for a cab. "It's a big section of the country."

"When are you supposed to pull out?" Steve asked. "And for where?"

"I'm supposed to pull for Chicago tonight."

"You loaded?"

Scotty glanced at his watch. "Should be by this time. I'd be surprised if they were holding a loading crew overtime. They quit at four, and it's three-thirty now. I figured to pull for Chicago about eleven tonight."

"How'd you like to leave now? By way of Lamar?"

"Suits me, buddy. I don't think I could sleep anyhow, not after this afternoon."

"I'll wheel the truck to Lamar, then you'll have a few hours before you hit for Chicago."

"How about me staying with you on this? I can re-plate some chrome or something, wire in that I'm out for repairs. I'll tell Ivy that I won't be home for a couple of days."

"Thanks, Scotty, but I've got a feeling that I'll need you worse in Salt Lake next week. That is if you can get a load for there."

"That's a breeze. Salt Lake runs go beggin' in the winter time. They even pay a fifty-buck bonus for takin' it."

"I'll leave a number at the terminal for you. That'll give you a chance to find me if I'm still in Salt Lake when you get there. It ought to be neater that way."

The two men had walked about eleven blocks when they finally caught sight of an oncoming cab. Steve hailed it and they went back to the hotel. Scotty went in, taking Steve's key, and emerged a few minutes later with the suitcase.

"Hell," he said, "did the law ever take that place apart. I imagine that this makes you hotter than a firecracker."

"Were they still there?"

"No. I went up to the fifth floor and then walked down to the fourth. The door to the room was still open—I guess they'd just left and hadn't posted a door guard yet, or something. Anyhow, I got the stuff out." Scotty was massaging the knuckles of his huge hand, and Steve got a picture of some young patrolman at his door taking an unexpected nap.

"They'll be looking for a Curt Blair, too. I imagine the prosecutor will put it all together, at least when this report goes into the hopper, and he finds a man turning up with a gunshot wound in my hotel room."

"You didn't use that name here, did you?" Scott asked.

"No, but except for my wallet, which was on me, the only name that could turn up would be that one, and that's one in which the federal attorney is going to be definitely interested."

"So now what do you do?"

"Like I told you before. We go to Lamar."

The cab slid up in front of the terminal where Scotty's truck sat in the yard. It was spotted under a different trailer—one containing eastbound freight. The trailer he had dropped lay next to it, still laden with the products of the East... looking strangely emasculated without the huge tractor. They paid the taxi driver and stepped into the yard. Steve slid into the truck while Scotty went for his clearance order. He was back in a few minutes and slid under the wheel. Steve had warmed the diesel, and they were underway in moments.

When they had cleared Denver and were skirting the mountains southward, Scotty laid the truck over to the roadside. "I'll take you up on that offer to wheel her. I do feel pretty beat."

The rest of the trip passed in silence. It was nearly five hours later when they reached the fork in the road that gave one communicating branch to the Rogers Ashe spread. Steve pulled the trucks to the pumps of the crossroads station and paid cash for a fill-up with diesel fuel. He slid out of the truck and put in a call to his father to pick him up. Then he returned to the cab and roused Scotty. The big man woke instantaneously with the road-conscious reflex of a driver. Then he looked at his watch.

"Good time, Steve. I guess you aren't out of practice too bad."

"I guess not. See you in Salt Lake, Scotty."

"I'll be there a week from today. Good hunting."

Steve swung the heavy door of the freighter and stood beside the truck until it came to life and racked away along the trail. The fading lights blinked five times in rapid succession—the highway code for "be careful." Suddenly he felt cold and alone. He turned into the lunch counter of the station to have people around and a mug of coffee during the short wait until Rogers Ashe could arrive.

CHAPTER TWENTY NINE

Steve was airborne at dawn, the little Culver he had borrowed chewing at the sky like an angry mosquito, ramming toward Denver. Jake Morris had supplied a terrain map for navigation, and an old resort map of the state. With a heavy pencil Steve had outlined nearly three dozen summer resorts within an hour's driving of Denver. If the hunch was right, Carazzi might be holed up in any of them, or perhaps any one of a dozen others.

While the Culver went on boring its tiny hole in the sky, he ran over the changes that had been instituted in the routine of the ranch. The plan of defense had been outlined for him late the night before by his father. Rogers Ashe was now going armed, just as he had forty years before when he came to the area. The guard chains of the heavy doors were now kept in place—even though they had not been slipped into the slots for all the time Steve could remember. Juana had a sharp, double-edged cuchillo in her garter. Even his mother had taken precautions. Martha Ashe was never far from a pistol. Juana's husband, Ramon, was stationed two hundred yards down the lane that led to the main house. He could fire the rifle jammed into the rack nailed on the large cottonwood tree by pulling a string. Rogers Ashe had sighted the gun in as he nailed on the rack. It would hit the old bell that had served years before to call the hands from the corral to their meals. The alarm system was good—the sound of a shot would be followed by the clang of the bell. This precaution was taken by Rogers Ashe in order to allow spring-awakened snakes or prowling coyotes to be shot .without the entire household springing to defense. Days were growing warm in the Arkansas Valley—it was well to consider these things.

The rolling swell of the Rocky Mountains appeared through the blur of the propeller in the thin morning light. Steve checked his map for landmarks. The rolling prairie with its tattered quilt of melting snow lay off to his right. Through the clear air he saw the pillar-like grain tanks of Limon, some forty miles to his right. Under his speeding wings the map-indicated terrain unfolded, the three gulches of Comanche, Bijou and Kiowa Creeks like scratches in the snow-covered grasslands of the upper plain.

He throttled back slightly and read his instruments, changing his course to cross the first spine of mountains just below the deserted resorts of Palmer Lake and the Glen. He circled both, noticing the accumulated snow had yet to feel the Kansas winds. He dipped lower to be certain. Except for the main highways and major streets of the village which had been plowed, there were no clear roads in the area. No smoke appeared above any of the cottages.

He clawed for altitude, topped little mountains and big trees. He wheeled and followed the highway to Denver, putting down at Arapahoe airport for refueling. Fifteen minutes later he was in the air again, cleared for Pueblo without the slightest intention of going there. He slid along the South Platte River, then wheeled west to begin a search of the Pike Forest area. He made dozens of wheeling swings in ten-mile arcs, using the twisting river and the equally twisting State Highway 75 as a baseline. He had calculated only that Carazzi must be within fifty miles of Denver, basing this estimate on the fact that they would not risk more than an hour on the road.

Hours passed. The little Culver had chewed up more than two-thirds of her gasoline. He had seen nothing unusual. There were no strange tracks off the highway, nor was there smoke from any of the summer cottages to guide him. He wheeled westward into the forest. Even in heavy gloves and flight jacket he felt chilled to the bone. The cockpit heater of the Culver was essentially useless in the high, thin, cold air near her service ceiling. Steve cursed sharply and wished that he had borrowed the Stinson. A radial engine at least threw heat, and wouldn't labor like a frantic hummingbird in thin air.

A few moments on the westerly course and the concrete expanse of Highway 285 was under him. He turned back toward Denver, looking for a place to put down before the Culver strangled on empty gas tanks and died a-weaning. A surprised attendant at a roadside service station watched the Culver touch down on the straight stretch of highway that fronted his station and taxi up to his gasoline pumps. He rubbed his eyes in disbelief, but the apparition refused to go away.

Steve had the tanks filled and rewarmed the engine. He produced a ten-dollar bill which stimulated the attendant to go around the curve at the far end of the station and stop oncoming traffic until the plane was in the sky again. The Culver spit angrily on the low-octane fuel, but rammed her way back into the air and grabbed space under her wings. Steve pointed her back toward Denver. The panel clock showed two. He had searched four hours, and in three more he would have to be clear of the shadow of the high hills. Off to his left was Brook Forest, lying deserted as only a summer resort can be deserted when the snow lies deep and cold. He turned for it, circling the area.

For the first time since he had left Denver he reached for the microphone and called. It was on the third try that he was able to raise an operator—the one at Idaho Springs.

"Idaho Springs."

"This is NC 9-7402. I want contact with the state police immediately."

"You're joking."

"No joke. This is an emergency. Please call them and have them monitor this frequency. Have them read this frequency—emergency!"

"Where are you, NC 9-7402?"

"Circling Brook Forest. Get the state police on this frequency, over."

It was perhaps five minutes, perhaps less, when another voice drummed into Steve's headset.

"State Police to NC 9-7402, come in."

"This is NC 9-7402. I have been conducting an air search for Mario Carazzi and two other men who escaped from Denver yesterday."

"Air search? Are you nuts? What the devil good would an air search be? They're probably still in Denver. We've had roadblocks stopping every car out of Denver for twenty-four hours."

"Listen, there is a possibility they made it out of Denver and are holed up. Carazzi is hurt, this I know. That's why the air search. I've found a single set of tracks and signs of life at a cottage four miles south of Brook Forest. I believe this is worth investigating."

"Who are you?"

"My name is Steve Ashe. If you doubt that I know what I'm talking about call the federal prosecutor in Denver. He'll tell you that I'm not crazy."

Another ten minutes went by, with the Culver narrowing its range around Brook Forest. Then the police operator was talking to him again.

"Ashe, the prosecutor wants you. Land at Idaho Springs immediately."

"Are you going to investigate Brook Forest?"

"Yes. There are two cars on the way."

"I'll lead them in. Then I'll call you back."

Steve whipped the Culver back along the route, settling low over it. He had raced over fifteen miles when he saw the two black and white cars top a ridge. He buzzed them, then stood the Culver on a wingtip to turn around. He throttled back to minimum, but still had to make three round trips to the target cottage and back to the cars before they drew up to the lane leading in. One car partially blocked the drive, and a trooper stayed beside it, tommy gun in hand. The other ground its way up the snowy inlet.

Steve wrapped the little craft into a tight circle and saw part of the action. His guess had been right. The figures of the little men looked like tiny animals from his height. He saw a trooper crumple from a shot from the house. Ugly red death spewed from a Thompson in the hands of one of the others. He dipped low over the house. Two men were coming out with their hands up. A third was draped over the railing of the cottage's porch. The trooper bearing the machine gun went into the house. Steve circled, watching. The trooper came out alone, and the cars began to move away.

A few moments later, when he felt the priority messages would have cleared the air, he called in again. It took a long time before the police operator was on his frequency again. He checked his maps and gas gauges.

"Ashe! NC 9-7402, NC 9-7402, come in!"

"Go ahead."

"Now get into Idaho Springs and land that thing."

"Did you get Carazzi?"

"No. He wasn't there. He'd been there, but he was gone—we don't know how."

"Get those jokers to talk, and find him!" Steve snapped.

"Don't give orders, mister…take 'em. Now get into Idaho Springs."

"I can't. I haven't enough gas left," Steve lied. "I'm gonna try and make Denver. I'll parallel Highway 285, in case I have to drop sooner."

There was a momentary pause, and then the operator cut back in. "All right," he said, "just get that thing in and land it."

Steve agreed, then released the microphone button and hung it back in the cradle. Immediately thereafter he pointed the plane west, away from Denver. His gasoline gauges indicated he had about two and one half hours of flying time. Leadville was over two hours away. He began a slow climb for altitude, praying that the little Culver had guts enough to clear the 11,000 feet of Belmont and Fremont Passes.

"Please Lord," he breathed, "no headwinds."

CHAPTER THIRTY

An hour before dawn, Steve broke out of the fitful slumber he had dropped into after making Leadville. He had racked out on a pile of parachutes in the only hangar of the tiny emergency field. He struck away the hand that shook his shoulder and leaped to his feet—temporarily out of contact with the reality of the strange and unfamiliar place. He looked about him, then back into the startled face of the mechanic who pulled the night shift in the emergency tower. Sheepishly he dropped his hands from their boxer's position.

"Sorry. I must have been dreaming," he admitted with a wry grin.

"Far as I'm concerned, you still could be, except that you asked me to call you. about five."

"My ship gassed up?"

"Yeah. Say, what's the capacity of that ship? She took almost twenty-four."

"The capacity? Twenty-four."

"You mean you made it over the pass on the fumes?"

"I guess so."

"Buddy, you got more guts than sense. How did you make it?"

"I dunno. I think I remember getting out and pushing over Fremont," Steve said drily.

The mechanic's wind-red face split into a grin. As suddenly as the incandescent grin had come it was gone. "What does the law want you for, mister?"

"Me? Nothing that I know of."

"Don't give me that. I got a receiver in the tower. All of the strips in the state have been posted to be on the lookout for a ship with those numbers. They got an air search putting out at dawn to find you somewhere in Pike Forest, but they aren't sure you didn't skip."

"Did you call in?"

"I ain't got no transmitter. Nothin' out here but a crank telephone, and it's been out for five days—ever since the last snow. I figured I'd drive into town this mornin' and find out what it was about."

Steve fumbled for his wallet. "Maybe this will help you lose your way goin' in."

"I don't want your money."

"It wasn't money I was digging for." Steve pulled out one of Jake Morris' business cards. On the back Jake had scribbled a note to the effect that any courtesy to his friend would be appreciated. Steve also had a list of a half-dozen fields in Colorado and west where Jake's note would work.

"I seen Jake Morris' name on that ship you rammed in here—that's why I figgered to take my time askin' the law about you. Only thing I can't figure is why you got his ship."

"Jake and I are both from Lamar … we flew fighters together out of England."

"Then you're Steve Ashe."

"Right."

"Jake's split a fistful of business our way, and when that guy lends an airplane to a friend it's gotta be somebody close. He ain't been in here for months but every time he does get in, your name comes up. Glad to meet you, Steve—I'm Tom Baldwin."

Steve put out his hand. "I guess you'd better know I didn't kill anybody. I just didn't want to be in protective custody until they got a grand jury into action. That might take weeks. I skipped because I'm a material witness in a case, and I got too many things to do to be sitting on the old dusty in jail."

"Well, like I say," the freckled man grinned, "I thought I'd get into town and report it sometime later this morning. How about a cup of coffee?"

"Good deal. Of course there's one other thing you'd ought to know. I'm signing to Lamar."

"Yeah…I know! But just off the record, when?"

"God knows. If I'm lucky I'll be back there within a month."

Fifteen minutes later, the thick black coffee still burning a spot in his belly, Steve rammed into the air. He buzzed the strip, then stood her on her tail to get the altitude necessary to take him over the hills to the west. When he hit six thousand he broke into the spread of sunshine that would be another fifteen minutes penetrating to the strip he had just left. The coffee warmth was fading out of his belly, and he was cold again. He maintained an on-course climb, pushing higher and higher to break the mountain barrier. His course was for Salt Lake City. It was three hours later when he pushed the tiny craft over the last lip of hills and swept down over the Utah flats.

At ten-fifteen he put the plane down on a small strip which Jake had listed. He was some twenty miles from downtown Salt Lake.

CHAPTER THIRTY ONE

March had touched Salt Lake City with wind. The air was sharp and clear as the high note of a flute solo, but the sun in the air set the calendar ahead some weeks. Flashing over the city a few minutes before, Steve had felt the radiated light from her white buildings and broad, symmetrical avenues. From the air the city had basked like a well-admired mistress of the sun. Now, from the dirty window of a battered taxi, she showed herself to be in need of cosmetics—the veneer showed a crack here and there.

Steve had no real plan for finding Gina. She could be just one face in perhaps a quarter-million faces. Of the quarter-million, half would be women—but only a small portion would be working prostitutes. That would narrow the field.

Steve checked into a hotel, bathed, shaved, and slept. At five in the afternoon, his clothes pressed by the hotel's valet service, he left. While most people were having their dinners, Steve was having breakfast. He put away a good meal, perusing the evening papers quickly.

When he had finished eating it was nearly six. He headed for the office of Salt Lake's morning newspaper, the Press. The lower floor of the building seemed asleep, except for the receptionist-switchboard girl. He paused at her counter for a moment.

"Jack Donnell still work for this outfit?" he inquired.

"Yes, he does, but I don't think he's in right now."

"Call him and tell him it's Steve Ashe, not a bill collector."

"I know he isn't in the office," she grinned over her headset. "I think I can locate him, but it might take a little while."

"How about Herb Matthews? Is he upstairs?"

"I believe so—do you want me to call and find out?"

"No. I'll go on up. He's still hacking with that pencil of his, isn't he?"

"Yes."

"And if you find Donnell, tell him I'll meet him for his lunch hour at Grady's at 8:30—I want to talk to him."

"Yes sir."

"Thanks, lover." Steve flipped the words over his shoulder as he climbed the imitation marble staircase to the editorial department.

Herb Matthews, bald spot ashine, was bent over a piece of copy in the center of the office when Steve entered the room. Several heads raised, then as the owners decided that this man was not going to provide a temporary interruption to their labors, dropped again to typewriters, handouts, and rewrites. Steve slipped into the chair opposite Matthews—the night city editor's slot. Matthews didn't look up.

"Where you been, Maxwell? You're late. Here, take these." The city editor flipped a sheaf of copy across the desk, still without looking up.

Steve took the copy and seized a pencil out of the jar. He scanned the copy quickly, knocking out a phrase here, a word there. Then he scratched a headline and flipped the copy back.

"Hey!" Matthews exploded, "we don't use balanced heads here—we use flush!" He looked up then and saw Steve's right hand resting on the center of the desk in a vulgar formation.

"Steve Ashe! Why you old son of a bitch, what in hell brings you to town?"

"Just poking, Herb. How you been?" Steve rose from the chair and went around the desk to Matthews' side, extending his hand. "I'm glad to see you're still here . What'd you do…find a home on this sheet?"

Matthews' florid face broke into a grin, and the little roll of fat under his jowls quivered with noiseless laughter. "I thought you were Ben Maxwell, the new NCE. His wife is due to pop any time now, and he thinks that's reason enough to be late almost every day."

"You old whip," Steve said, "you'd probably think it was too, if it was your wife."

"Yeah, I suppose I would." Matthews' tone modified. "But I got past that years ago. My boy's eleven now—the youngest one, that is. He just had a birthday last week. He was born just after I took the desk of the old Transcript."

"And three years before you had a rookie reporter named Steve Ashe."

"You sure were a dumb one, too. Couldn't have poured it out of a boot with the directions printed on the heel." Matthews sat back, jiggling with his joke. Suddenly he sobered and leaned forward with an interested look. "You looking for a job?"

"No."

The chunky little editor's face fell perceptibly. "Nuts! I thought maybe we'd get a reporter on the rag for a change."

"Someday—maybe soon, but not now. I'm just kind of passing through."

"Who you working for?"

"Nobody. I'm hunting for somebody."

"And you want help ... naturally. I should know that you're coming in to see me would have a hook in it somewhere."

"I could use some help. About six weeks ago a young girl was white-slaved in here from Denver. She's only seventeen and on the needle. The kid is hooked and hooked deep. I want to find her, and the quicker the better."

"That's a pretty tall order. It wouldn't have been so tough a week ago, but then the heat went on—and things are runnin' considerably different around here now."

"How different?"

"Well, all the regular notch-houses are runnin' under wraps. Most of the girls that are working are the call trade. Of course, the heat just moved 'em all out to the suburbs, outside the corporate limit. Only trouble with calling for them is that you might be here six months and never get the right one. There's probably a couple of hundred."

"Call girls have to have some appointment center. Somebody rides the phone for them."

"Yeah—that's true. I only know of three possibilities, but I imagine that Jack Donnell could give you a list as long as your arm."

"Give me the three," Steve said.

"All I know is the numbers and some names."

"Didn't you even check 'em out in your cross-index?"

Matthews grinned again. "If you had a wife like Edna," he said, "you wouldn't be interested in how to get hold of a madam either."

Now it was Steve's turn to grin, and his face split with the ludicrous picture of Edna Matthews, with her solid stability and easy acceptance of man's foibles and failings, growing suddenly irate over the dim possibility of her husband becoming a habitual user of professional prostitutes.

"I guess you're right," Steve said. He took the list that Matthews had penciled out on a piece of copy paper, then dug into the drawer for the cross-index listings. All that the index gave was the names attached to telephone numbers. He jotted them down, then looked up the names in the regular directory to get the addresses.

"The names can be phony as a three-dollar bill," Matthews said, "but the addresses have to check."

"You don't have to tell me," Steve said, "you trained me."

Jack Donnell breezed into the office then, almost on a run. He was tall and squarely built, like a Percheron, and you somehow expected to see him with a massive briar and a tweed jacket with chamois reinforcements at the elbows and shoulders. He crossed the room to grab Steve's hand and wrung it savagely. After the usual quota of profanity and expressions of surprise, Donnell expanded the list of phone numbers to seven names. Steve collected the seven addresses, and found they were all lodged in three buildings.

"Three places?" Donnell said quizzically. "Maybe we got more of an organization of pimps in this town than we know, Herb. One thing I do know, there's just three standard prices in this town—of course they'll take all the traffic will bear—they go at twenty, fifty and a hundred, with overnights and weekends somewhat higher."

"I'd give you sis, two, and even that it's all the same outfit," Steve said. He filled the two men in on the Denver situation, including the message center and the methods of operation.

When the conversation fell back to the specific item of Gina Marotti, Donnell had a question. "How long has this kid been on junk?" he asked.

"About three or four months," Steve said.

"And she's a looker?"

"Yes."

Donnell pulled on his chin. "She'd probably still be in the hundred-dollar-and-up bracket, then. The dope wouldn't have caught up with her yet and she'd have her looks for a couple of months yet. What did she look like—a real hormone shuffler?"

"You can say that again. She's blonde, really terrific. Stands about five-four and weighs maybe 120 with all of it in the right places."

Matthews joined in. "You suppose she's still a blonde?" he, asked.

"Who knows? I imagine that she is—it would be one of her strong points, and she was a couple of weeks ago anyhow." Steve looked up at the two men quizzically. "If you were me," he asked, "how would you go about finding her?"

"I dunno," Donnell admitted. "I suppose you're in plenty of a hurry too."

"If I don't get to her before Carazzi, she'll be dead." Steve spoke the words implying pressure almost automatically. "Yeah, I'm in a hurry—too much of a hurry to just play these numbers until I'd get her sent to me. That was my first idea—to just start asking for blondes. Like you say, though, she might be another color by now—especially if somebody wanted to hide her out."

"You think that's what Carazzi might have had in mind?"

"He knew her sister was out looking for her after she got away from Omaha. He'd told her about chaining Gina in a crib in Salt Lake—bragged to her sister about it. If she were to come looking she might find her—so Carazzi might hide her out."

"Maybe she isn't even in Salt Lake anymore."

"I thought of that, too."

"What happens if she isn't here?" Matthews asked.

"I don't know. I do know that the big wheel of this Outfit's in Los Angeles. Maybe that would be where they'd take her if the heat went on."

"That's an easy town to get lost in," Donnell interposed. "Out there they don't ask any weird questions about who's shacking up with you. Just pay your rent and don't let your customers get too loud."

The sentence hit Steve hard. He supposed that in a way he hadn't even thought of Gina in that way—with the prostitute's inevitable customer. He had objectively known it, but he hadn't felt it until now. His back teeth ground together. He licked his lips and felt anger rising in his belly, forcing perspiration out into his palms.

Matthews was fumbling under the desk. From some recess of a lower drawer he brought three paper cups and set them out on the desk without a word. Steve looked up at him, noticing the further recession of the hairline and the deeper squint that had marked the nine years since they had been mentor and student.

Matthews hadn't changed, Steve decided, he still knew when to pour a drink. The three men tipped up and drained the heavy blasts of Scotch.

"I've been thinking," Matthews said. "If you need it, we can get together a dozen or so guys and start a stag party, then send for a dozen blondes. There couldn't be too many in the hundred-buck class in this little town, and we might find her that way—quick."

Steve looked up, the glimmer of an idea breaking through, as Matthews went on. "Also," the editor said, "it would be a lot safer than trying to knock over three phone boards in the hopes of finding her. They've got a muscle team that operates around here, and it isn't a soft one either. Even if you didn't get nailed, they'd get her out if they could know where you were going to look before you got there."

"It might work," Steve said, "but would that wallop be something we could work tonight?"

"Why not?" Donnell broke in. "We ought to be able to get five or six guys right here on the staff, then with the three of us and a couple of more, we'd make it. For a couple of hours with a hundred-dollar broad we'd probably get the whole town."

Matthews looked up at Donnell. "Good enough idea," he said, "but where's the dough comin' from?"

Steve answered that one. "Carazzi," he said, "I still got some of his dough. I can finance about ten guys and still have enough left if I have to go on to L.A." He grinned Inwardly at the prospect of letting Carazzi's stable of fillies—earn the same money for the second time.

"If we could find some way to team it up with a real story," Matthews interjected, "the paper'd probably pick up the tab without too much squawk."

"There's a story there, all right, but it won't break until we pin the big guy—that is it won't be broken on more than a local level until then."

"Will you do it?" Matthews asked, looking directly at Steve.

"You mean, will I cover it?"

"I want ten running articles, I'll pay a hundred a chunk for exclusive and wire rights under your by-line. Every article is one more girl you can look over tonight."

"You just hired yourself a reporter. I won't file any copy until the whole story is complete—then you can sell it any way you please."

Matthews' wrinkled face exploded into a 200-watt grin. "Holy sufferin' Maggie!" he exclaimed. "Maybe I'll finally be able to sell something to L.A. that happens right in their own back yard. It'd be worth five thousand just for the chance to do that." He sat back deep in the chair, a chuckle bubbling around in his throat.

CHAPTER THIRTY TWO

The party progressed in the confused babble of men with nothing to talk about and some desperate eagerness to talk about it. The group had been drinking since Matthews had folded up the desk and left it in the hands of the NCE at 10:30. That is, the guests were drinking. Steve, Matthews, and Donnell nursed drinks, ditched them, gave them away, did anything but work on the bottles. Matthews was putting on a good act of being the hale fellow well met. He achieved so much success at this role that no one was surprised by his suggestion that women be sent for. It seemed like the normal outcome of this kind of party, and as always when someone else was to pay the freight, the freeloaders were much in favor.

"Jus' one thing," Matthews growled to the assembled company in a good imitation of a tongue-thick drunk. "This whole party is for my friend Steve. Therefore I think it only fitting and proper that he gets his pick of all the girls—then the rest of us'll take our chances on what's left."

Matthews had done well. The party had organized itself almost without effort and was underway by eleven. Now, at midnight, it was in good shape for its part in the operation. They were in the small banquet room of one of Salt Lake's not-so-plush hotels. A dozen or more room keys lay on the table.

The babble of voices competed for attention again as Steve, Matthews, and Donnell stepped into the lobby to make phone calls for women.

"Have you got those sleeping pills?" Steve asked.

Donnell reached into his coat pocket and produced a box of seconal tablets. "This won't really help much when she starts going 'cold.' She'll be hell on wheels if she's hooked as you say."

"I know it." Steve spoke slowly, a wire-edge of sadness raking his voice. "There's no other way, though—at least right now—without bringing somebody else into the thing. How about the car?"

"I'll drive you," Donnell said, "if you find her. Where'd you say the plane was?"

Steve told him the location of the small strip where the little Culver would be refueled and ready to go at a moment's notice. Donnell said it would take about twenty minutes to get there.

"Let's go over it again," Matthews said. "Steve will pick the girl to her left and take her up to Room 802. Then Jack, you'll grab the girl we want and take her to 804. I'll come there and we'll hold her until Steve gets rid of the other one. By this time all the guys should be racked out with the others, so we make it out the side door and into the car. Right from there we go to the airport."

"That's it," said Steve, looking at the watch he had borrowed from Jake Morris along with the plane. "Now I think you'd better make the calls, Jack. Remember, insist on young ones, not over twenty-five, and get as many blondes as you can."

"Right." Donnell slipped into the phone booth on the mezzanine just outside the banquet room. In about three minutes he was back with the old editor and Steve. "I did better than I expected," he said. "Martha will send over twenty so we can take our pick."

"That boosts the odds," Steve said. "Now I guess we'd better get back to the party."

They returned to the jungle of noise in the banquet room and passed along the information that women would show up in a few minutes. They had been gone less than fifteen minutes, yet sobriety was a thing of the past. For the three of them, nearly cold sober, it was not the most pleasant of gatherings. They made a pretense of having another drink, and joined in the telling of lewd stories. Under cover of an. outburst of raucous laughter, Donnell drew Steve aside.

"What are you going to do if she recognizes you and yells?" he asked.

Steve thought a moment. This angle hadn't occurred to him. "That's right! I guess the best way out would be to pat her on the butt and say I'd get around to her later. What we've got to do is to make sure that there's plenty of noise going on and that she gets cut out of the crowd of women pretty pronto. Any diversion is up to you and Herb."

"You know they'll have somebody riding herd on them, don't you?"

"Yeah, I know. Here's hoping that we make it." Steve drained the half-finished drink he had toyed with for the twenty minutes they had been back in the room. He felt it hit. His time in vigorous training had made him unused to alcohol. He reached for a bottle and tilted it, pretending to pour a huge drink. Then he filled the glass with soda. He could drink this all night.

Donnell and Steve turned back to the conversation. The jokes went on, whetting the men's appetites for nearly half an hour more. Then the girls began to arrive in twos and threes. They joined in, drank, laughed uproariously at the jokes, and gathered little knots of men around them ... knots which would partially dissolve as each new girl arrived. There were eleven now. Gina was not among them. Steve and Donnell circulated throughout the room, waiting and hoping.

Hawkins, a small and highly belligerent man, began to feel the urge. "What are we waiting for?" he yelled.

"The rest of the girls," Steve answered, "I want to see 'em all. Just keep your pants on—they'll be here."

The little man had a lissome brunette by the wrist. He reached for one of the room keys on the table. "I got what I want—see you all later."

It was the signal for a stampede. If one of them got out of the room they'd scatter like cattle. It was Herb Matthews who rose to the occasion.

"I told you," he yelled, "my buddy is gonna get the pick of all of 'em. I'll admit you got an eye for a good-looker, Charlie, but you aren't playin' the game. I'm pickin' up the tab, so what I say goes—unless you want to pay your own freight. Sit down and have a drink—she ain't gonna run away."

The little man, sobered by the threat to his own pocket-book, sat down heavily and pulled the brunette into his lap. "You're still for me, baby," he said in a voice that was meant to warn all comers. She patted his ears and looked across at Steve and Donnell with the shrug that indicated this was all in a day's work.

More girls were coming in. Steve kept his face averted and held to the opposite end of the room from the door. He scanned each face intently as the girls came in. It wasn't until the seventeenth girl arrived that he saw Gina. For a moment he almost failed to recognize her. She looked tired, artificial. Her eyes were dull and hopeless. She picked up her job, making small erotic noises amid a little knot of men, laughing, joking, and automatically going through a soundless sales talk. She hadn't really seen anyone in the room.

The last one of the girls arrived and had a drink shoved into her hand. Steve continued to busy himself at the other end of the room, talking to a leggy, red-haired girl who missed being beautiful by a trifle too much nose.

"Who's the little blonde?" he asked.

"Her?" The redhead's glance went to Gina. "Her name's Karen, I think. I knew you'd notice her. I'd have bet on it —you got taste."

"You stand next to her, doll, and see which one I pick."

"She'll get your nod, handsome. I'll bet on that, too."

"How much?"

"Nothing. For a couple of bucks you'd choose Mrs. Dracula herself."

"Mrs. Dracula?"

"That long blonde witch over at the end of the trail," the girl said. "She's here to make sure you're all paying customers."

"Oh," he said in three tones, "the shop steward."

"Yeah, isn't she the motherly type?" The girl laughed bitterly. "Another three or four years the little blonde deal you asked about could look just like her. That is she could if she wasn't..."

"Wasn't what?"

"...I don't know," said the redhead. "Gonna work herself to death, maybe. She takes eight or ten tricks a night. Most of us just work. She slaves at it."

"Maybe she loves her work?"

"Maybe." The redhead's eyes went soft for a flickering instant. "She doesn't look like she belongs in this racket," she added.

Steve nodded. "I guess she doesn't... but then neither do any of you."

"We come high-priced, mister. Who would want soiled-looking merchandise? Of course we don't fit some hell-fire preacher's stereotype—not in looks, in action, or in speech."

"Don't get hot about it, Red... I'm no blue nose out for a wild night."

It was then that Matthews beckoned. Steve nodded to the girl. "Don't forget what I told you about standing next to the kid and seeing who I'd pick—just for laughs."

"All right, you got a bet. You haven't seen her up close yet. She's a real attraction." She rose from her chair and wandered off across the room.

Matthews came up and Steve gave him the layout. "Now's the time, Herb. The girl's here. Just one thing, get that long lean blonde at the end of the table out of circulation. She's the spotter. Take her out in the hall right now. Talk money—anything, but get her out of here. When she's out, Jack will line 'em up and we'll move."

"O.K., Steve." Matthews jammed his hand in his pocket and came up with the sheaf of bills Steve had given him in exchange for the check bearing the name of the newspaper and the disbursal-for-feature-articles label. There had been no other way for Matthews to have the cash that night, and in one profession all transactions had been for cash since ancient Babylonia.

The editor crossed the room and whispered a few words into the blonde's ear. She nodded and went with him to the corridor. As they cleared the room, Donnell asked all of the girls to line up to be looked over. The men also rose, and the two lines faced each other across the room.

The redhead was as good as her word. She moved in line until she was standing next to Gina. The two girls stood out among the others. Donnell came to Steve.

"Here we go, buddy," he breathed.

"Stay on my right," Steve cautioned, "she's the girl on the right, not the left." He crossed the room quickly and took the redhead by the wrist. Gina looked up, startled, with recognition breaking in her eyes. She started to call his name. Donnell rose to the occasion. He closed her mouth in the only gentlemanly way—with his own.

Gina found herself being pulled along by Donnell, toward the door. She heard his voice hammering at her in an almost soundless whisper. "Don't yell, you little fool," he breathed, "we're friends."

CHAPTER THIRTY THREE

Not until they had left the elevator and were in the eighth-floor corridor alone, did the redhead speak. She was stretching her long legs to match Steve stride for stride. She stood tall, erect, and almost proud. When she did speak, her voice was firm and mellow.

"Why didn't you take the little blonde?" she inquired.

"I like you better, Red. You look like a lot of woman," Steve answered, turning the pass key in the door. They entered the room. Steve turned the key in the lock inside while she stepped across the room and sat on the edge of the bed.

"Maybe I am, mister, but the blonde is young and fresh."

"And on the needle."

"How did you know?"

"Her eyes. She must have had a jolt in the last two hours."

"Yeah. You would notice. I don't suppose that one guy in a hundred would, but you would. Still, I wonder why you didn't take her anyhow. Are you afraid of a hop?"

"No. Like I say, I had eyes for you."

The redhead shrugged it off, dismissing the conversation. "Well, let's go to bed," she said, rising from the edge of the bed and stretching sensually. She peeled off the jacket of her trim business suit and draped it neatly over a chair back. Her breasts were firm and unrestrained.

Steve was playing for time. He had to make sure that they wouldn't have other members of the party in the halls until it would be less obvious for him to leave the redhead. He began fumbling with his tie. "How do you feel about the kid—any kid like that—being on the needle?"

"I hate the thought of the stuff," the prostitute answered simply. "I wish there was some way to help that kid." Her skirt fell around her ankles as she answered. Steve revised his estimate. She was really quite beautiful. Her body was lithe and supple, and her legs were long and slender. The rolling curves of her hips blended into a board-flat belly.

"That's what the party was for," he said, "just to help that kid. We're getting her out and into a hospital."

The redhead looked up at him, pausing in her professional job of folding the skirt. Then she sat back on the edge of the bed and began to laugh. "I should have known," she said, "guys like you don't have to buy anything."

"You'll get paid. We had to stage the party to find this girl. Now the weird question is, what are you going to do about it?"

"Not a thing, except enjoy it." She went on in quiet mirth, merriment rippling across her chest and setting her breasts aquiver like a pair of young colts.

"I wish I could trust you, Red."

"What makes you think you can't?"

"I've seen this outfit work before." Steve crossed the room to the bed and stood in front of her. He took her head in his hands and raised her to her feet. He kissed her, long and hard. "You're probably all right, Red," he said, "but I can't take the chance." His thumbs were under her chin, and his fingertips under her ears. He pressed hard with both for perhaps ten seconds. The arteries to her brain were closed. She passed out. Gently he laid her back onto the bed, and with a short chopping right to her now slack jaw, he insured her being unconscious long enough for the four of them to get away.

Before he left the room he laid two hundred dollars across her jacket and turned to leave the room. For a moment, at the door, he paused and looked back. She was one of the few women who actually look their best nude. The twin foals of her breasts were rising and falling smoothly and evenly, and he felt a twinge of regret somewhere deep in his loins. Then he was out of the room and knocking on the door of the room down the hall.

When Matthews opened the door, Gina was sitting in a deep chair, looking frightened. As Steve entered she tried to rise and Donnell, standing behind the chair, caught her shoulders and pushed her back down again.

"Steve," she said uncertainly, "what is this? What's going on?"

"We're getting you out of here."

"I'm not going anywhere. I like it here." She said the words defiantly, but the lost look came back into her face and her mascara-trimmed eyes began to mist up.

"Just one question, Gina. How big is your habit?"

"What do you mean, habit?"

"Don't kid me. Vicki told me you were on narcotics. Now, how deep are you hooked?"

"I'm not hooked, I can quit anytime."

"You're going to get the chance. I'm taking you out of here right now."

"I like it here," she began, "and I don't need any help from you or anybody else. As for Vicki, she's just another one who didn't know a good thing when she saw it..."

Steve's slap took her across the face and she crumpled into the chair, crying softly. "I'm not going to argue with you, Gina," he said. "You've been needing a butt-warming for a long time, but we don't have the time or the space to waste. Get on your feet. We're getting out of here!"

She rose, dazedly. Steve shoved three seconal tablets at her. "Take these," he snapped, "because you've had your last* jolt—ever."

The anticipation terrified her, and terror wrought ugliness into every line of her face. "No!" she spit the words at him. "I'm not going anywhere with you."

"Take your choice. You can go with me, or you'll go to jail and a prison hospital as a habitual narcotics user. I'm through giving in to you, kid. You're going to do what you're told, and right now." He shoved the tablets at her viciously. "Take these!"

"No."

Steve grasped her wrist and twisted her around. He pinned her shoulders against his chest. With his free hand he forced her mouth open by pressing her cheeks against her teeth. She writhed against him, aflame with anger. Donnell stepped up and took the seconal tablets from the hand on her shoulders. He forced them into her mouth and clamped her jaws shut. Steve's left hand moved from the sides of her jaws to her nose, closing the nares. In a few seconds she swallowed convulsively, and the two men loosened their grip.

"Like giving a worm tablet to a stubborn puppy," Matthews observed drily, "except that you didn't have to stroke her throat. How long before those things work?"

"It'll be a little while, but we won't wait for that. Jack, you go down and get the car around to the side entrance. We'll be down just—" Steve glanced at his watch— "eight minutes from now."

Gina twisted in his grasp until she could look at him. Her eyes were widening unevenly with fright and the strictures of heroin. "Steve," she pleaded, "don't take me away. Don't do it to me. I've tried to stop. But I can't. I just can't. I've got to have it … don't take me away."

He slapped her again, harder, then put her back into the chair. "Listen, you little fool," he grated at her, "the crumb who hooked you, Carazzi, jammed the needle to Vicki too. It almost killed her. She broke it herself. She locked herself in a stable for four days to break it. She fought and won. Then they tried to kill her, tried to ruin your folks—they tried everything."

"I don't care what's happened. You don't know what it's like, you couldn't. I've got to have it. I've tried. How I've tried!"

"How big is your habit?"

"Forty dollars a day."

Matthews looked at Steve in amazement. "Good Lord," he exclaimed, "forty a day!" He swung his gaze to Gina, "How much do you make on this call racket?"

"I've got to pull four tricks to have anything left. I only get twenty bucks a trick. They've got me cold. All the other girls get sixty, but if I ask for it they tell me they'll cut off my supply."

"All right, now talk," Steve snapped, "who supplies you?"

"Nobody."

"You aren't going to get any more of it—who is it? You're going to tell me if I have to beat it out of you."

"Larry Kenner comes in from Denver once a month. He gives some to Leah for me. When I'm heavy, I get it from Jerry Saxton, too. Kenner supplies him from Denver."

"Who's Leah?"

"The booker. She's the tall blonde who was at the table just before we broke up downstairs."

"I know Saxton," Matthews broke in, "a no-account if ever there was one. I'll take care of him. Now for God's sake let's get out of here."

Steve glanced at his watch. "Yeah," he said, "it's time." He pulled Gina to her feet and slipped his arm under her shoulders. The seconal hadn't really hit her yet, but it wouldn't be long. She was unsteady on her feet and reeled more the further down the hall they progressed.

In the elevator, Gina entered the drowsy stage. Her voice blurred and her motion to straighten a lock of her hair was grossly inaccurate. Steve made conversation for the benefit of the elevator operator. Matthews continued his drunk act. They looked like debris from the kind of a party they were supposed to have had. Gina tried to say something, but her words from the borderline of sleep and consciousness ran together.

They were in the car for perhaps a minute when she slumped against Steve's shoulder. She was out cold.

CHAPTER THIRTY FOUR

Steve warmed the engine of the little Culver, then shut it off and had the night mechanic at the airport fill the tank with the gasoline he had burned up in the minutes of insurance time against engine failure. The ship took two gallons, which might mean the difference between making Leadville or breaking up on some jagged crest, a flaming streak in the cold night sky.

Matthews and Donnell were at the end of the airstrip. After they had taken Steve to the airport, they had driven back down the road to the end of the field. It was there that they waited, with Gina Marotti sleeping peacefully in the back seat.

The sleepy air control manager took a look at the sheet that Steve had just signed. "H. Mahogany Maxwell!" he said. "You're going to pull a cross country at maximum range over the desert and start at this time in the morning?"

"I've got to be in Phoenix in the morning," Steve answered. "My sister's sick—gonna be operated on. I got to get there. I've flown for two days. When I got here I had to hang up until I could get a little rest. I didn't want to take the chance of racking up somewhere out there."

"Yeah. I know what you mean. Well, good luck to you."

"I'll clear tower from the end of the runway. I gotta be sure of my magnetos. I'll give 'em a long check and wait for any incoming traffic."

"Incoming traffic? At one-fifty A.M.? You sure got the wrong idea about this runway."

"Thanks for the good job your boys did. She sounded pretty when I warmed her." Steve nodded toward the plane.

"You need more than a light overhaul on that bucket," the man said. "The way those plugs were fouled you're sucking oil like water. You ought to be glad you don't have to push very high to get over the ridges. If you were going east over the hog-back you might not make it."

"Yeah—especially if there were ice."

"There would be, going east. Right down the middle hump is a stationary cold front. It set in about two-thirty this afternoon. They cleared commercial stuff up to thirty thousand."

"Yeah, that'd be real great. This bucket mushes out at about twelve—and there isn't any oxygen. I'm glad I'm going to Phoenix." Steve said the words with a smile, but there was the familiar knot of fear in his stomach. With ice on the wings and Gina's extra one hundred and twenty pounds, the little plane might pull twelve thousand feet. It might not. There was no clear air in the altitude he could play around in except for the twenty or thirty feet above the actual ground surface unless the weather report was wrong. If he iced up, he would have only one way to go … down into that narrow belt. At night, with responsibility for a life other than his own, it was not going to be a picnic. He climbed into the cockpit.

The pre-warmed engine caught easily under the impact of the freshly cleaned spark-plugs. He taxied slowly to the end of the runway, swung the ship to a forty-five degree angle and stomped the brakes into lock. Then he jumped out of the plane.

Matthews and Donnell had seen his clearance lights approaching on the slow taxi run. They lifted Gina from the car and put her through the barbed wire fence at the end of the strip. Steve helped them load the unconscious girl into the plane.

"She may come out of it," he yelled over the racket of the idling engine. "Give me your belts."

They ripped the belts from their waistbands, and Steve lashed the girl's ankles to the frame of the seat. He forced her limp arms back over the seat and tied them at the wrists. No matter how hard withdrawal hit her, she wouldn't be in his way. He set the heavy webbing of the safety belt around her stomach and drew it tight. He didn't like tying her, but getting over the ridge without plowing a sudden furrow in the pines would be difficult enough. If he should have to deal with Gina's withdrawal hysteria, it would be impossible. He closed the right-hand door and jumped off the wing. As he came around the plane, Matthews and Donnell were waiting for him.

"Steve," Matthews said, "forget the articles."

"You'll get them. That is, you'll get them if I can get the story."

"It was worth it. We'll get plenty of local stories on this and burn tails around city hall as it is."

"I know you will. Take your time and make sure they're all in the net before you break line one."

Jack Donnell grasped his hand. "Take it easy, Steve."

"No other way, Jack." Steve pumped the man's hand, then clasped Matthews' shoulder while he shook his hand. "So long, Herb. You'll be hearing from me." He was glad his face was shielded in the dark. "Thanks—thanks a million, fellas."

Steve turned quickly and threw a leg up onto the wing of the tiny plane. He grasped the canopy and pulled the door open, waving a brief salute to the two men, then he turned to the business at hand. He ran the engine up and checked the two magnetos. The pressure gauges and sound of the engine indicated the Culver was in good shape. He breathed a silent prayer that his ear still knew the sound of a good engine. Then he reached for the microphone and asked for clearance.

"O.K., NC 9-7402—it's all your runway. Latest weather between here and Phoenix is clear and cold, no icing conditions. Wind at 290, eight miles per hour. How are your mags?"

"Good and clear," Steve answered, "no drop in pressure and minimum loss of rpm. Should be a cakewalk."

"Good sail."

"Thanks."

The little Culver pulled into the air. Steve hauled the gear up away from the runway, keeping her low along the strip for speed. He stood her on her tail and grabbed a handful of sky. He laid into a 190 degree bearing and let his tiny marker lights fade, looking back to see the airstrip lights receding in the cold clear night. When they ran into an indistinct blur he switched off his running lights and bent the ship to the 93 degree heading that would take him back to Leadville. It was nearly ten minutes later when he flipped the little toggle switch that brought the three lights back on. Behind were the lights of Salt Lake, a dim glow in the night.

The first hour was easy, but then he began to feel cold and the thin air was making him a little giddy. He cursed the drinks he had taken, shaking his head to clear the fuzz from his thoughts. He pulled the map-light, and the cockpit flared with the sudden brilliance. The map on the clipboard got a pair of pencil marks. He still had more than three hundred miles to go. He eased back on the wheel, trying for a little more altitude. The ship felt heavy and unresponsive.

Matthews had insisted they stop for coffee on the way to the airport, and Steve was thankful for it now. He reached for the package between the seats, an insulated bag, meant to hold ice-cream, but capable of keeping a quart bottle of coffee fairly hot. Steve gulped two mouthfuls of. the bitter coffee, then fitted the soggy cap back into the top of the bottle and jammed it back into the sack.

The plane burst over the first ridge of the mountains. To the left he saw the lights of Junction City. Then the airspeed needle dropped and quivered. The altimeter began to unwind. Instead of the clean racket of the engine, he heard the choppy, stick-down-a-picket-fence rattle of a laboring airplane. He eased off slightly, and the Culver began to lose altitude. Waggling the ailerons and moving the flaps with the little crank, he tried to shed the ice.

Finally above the racket of the engine he heard the pistol-shot snaps of breaking ice. He tried the wheel again, and the Culver responded. He throttled back to a point just below cruising and prayed that he could react fast enough to miss the moonlit slopes.

There was a bare thirty feet between the belly of the Culver and the slopes. He spotted jagged heights and circled them. It was a battle of watch and altimeter. "One and a half minutes at 30 degrees, one minute at 140, then resume the 93 degree heading." He was saying these things to himself constantly, each peak presenting a different problem. There was no possibility of going over them. He went around. At five minutes after three he picked up the radio beam out of Denver on the under-powered little radio. He thanked God for a constant reference.

The caps of the mountains ahead in the east began to bleach with light. Steve had about one hundred miles to go. He bent to check his gas gauges. It was at that moment that Gina began to awake with the first cramps and horror of narcotics withdrawal.

It started with a slow moaning. Her over-extended nervous system, lashed to the inflexible time-schedule of heroin, brought her back to consciousness like a throbbing toothache. She lurched forward in the seat, belt-bound wrists dragging against the metal frame. At the moment she was aware of nothing but her pain. Her muscles and glands racked under its twist. Tears streamed down her face.

Steve noted the compass heading. In the moonlight he saw a long valley ahead. He left the ship on course, and wrenched the coffee bottle from the insulated bag. With his right arm around Gina's shoulders and his knees up, locking the wheel in position, he brought the bottle to her lips with his left hand. She swallowed automatically, excess coffee running off her chin onto the twisted lapels of Matthews' heavy overcoat. He gave her more. She choked, spewing coffee against the instrument panel. Slowly consciousness came upon her. She twisted her shoulders and looked at him. In her fog of seconal it took Her a full minute to recognize him. Even then she did not realize the situation.

"You ... you're Steve," she said, "Uncle Steve."

"Yeah," he answered, "go back to sleep."

"My very good friend ... my ... love." She drifted away.

"Go to sleep, Gina mia. Go to sleep." He laid the Culver over into a steep climbing turn. Gina rocked sideways, shuddering to a stop when her arms hit the back of the seat.

Steve finished checking the gauges. He had gasoline—nearly half of capacity—but he didn't know how far off course he was. He looked at the map again, then at the luminous face of the chronograph. With luck he would be able to make it within an hour, but the biggest of the ridges he would have to overcome was still before him. Gina stirred again and wakened to terror.

"Steve!" she screamed, "what are you doing?"

"Taking you home," he answered. "Everything will be all right. Just be quiet. Go back to sleep."

"But we're flying, and it's cold and dark."

"Go to sleep. It'll be all right." Steve found the lie catching in his throat. He had to reach over eleven thousand feet to slip into the Salida Valley, and he had little faith that he could do it.

Withdrawal cramps hit Gina hammer blows. The coffee she had taken hit the instrument panel in a spurt. She retched deep inside, the great gagging sounds audible even above the laboring engine of the airplane. She wrenched forward in the seat. A tiny stream of spittle ran from the corner of her mouth. Steve fished for a handkerchief to mop her face. Her body contorted, jerking against the straps that held her. She went rigid. Her spasm broke into a minor convulsion.

"I'm sick," she cried. "I'm sick—I've got to have a fix." She turned her head toward him and almost screamed. "I've got to have a fix—in my purse. In my purse I've got a kit. Let me have it, please."

"No!"

"In my purse," she screamed. "I've got to have it … I've got to!" She strained against the belts. "Anything, I'll give you anything! Look at me—I'm pretty—how about me? Please, please—just a little jolt—I'm so sick." She swung her legs against the straps, the airplane vibrating as she lunged. "All the way, honey—all the way, any way you want me." She threw her head back, and lunged again.

The next few minutes lost all rationality: Gina fought and strained against her bonds. She cursed in English and Italian. Steve flew the Culver on, watching her when he could steal a look.

Gasping for air, she quieted for a moment. In that moment he faintly caught the A signal of the Denver beam again, and began easing the Culver left. He saw a pair of lights top a ridge as a lumbering truck dragged itself over a mountain highway. He pulled open the map-board. The truck must be on Route 6. By his best calculations he was north of Bald Mountain, and south of Glenwood Springs.

For a moment Steve thought that Gina had lost consciousness again, and was glad. It would be less painful that way. Then she lunged forward again. The leather belt that had bound her wrists gave with a ripping sound. She grabbed for the wheel in front of her. Steve grasped his set of the controls tightly, braced against her fury.

"I want that stuff," she yelled. "I want it right now—I've got to have it."

"No!" he yelled back. "Let go, you'll kill us both!"

"I don't care. Give me the stuff!"

One look at her was enough. For the moment she was psychotic, driven by the terror of withdrawal. She was willing to take the little plane to destruction. She was eager to die to escape the pain.

"All right," Steve yelled, "you win. I'll get it, it's behind the seat."

"Now. Right now!"

"All right. I'll get it. Just don't move that wheel." Steve forced himself to do the hardest thing he had ever done. He took his hands off the wheel and turned in the seat. The Culver's nose dipped. He put his hands down toward her purse. In the rack behind the seat his fingers closed over a small magnesium flare. He pulled it to seat height and swung. It caught Gina behind the left ear and she slumped forward, driving the wheel into the instrument panel and pointing the Culver in a screaming dive toward the floor of a valley.

Steve whirled back in the seat and grasped his wheel. He hauled back, lifting Gina's weight from the other wheel. The snow-covered slopes were rushing to envelope them. Torturously the little Culver pulled back into a level attitude. Before him rose the specter of a moon-shadowed cliff. He yanked back the wheel, twisted it, and kicked full right rudder almost automatically. The Culver's broad stubs of wings pressed at the thin air. Then they held. The ship heeled over and broke away from the cliff.

Slowly Steve fought the Culver up. When the ship was out of danger and on course, he picked up the microphone and began trying to raise Leadville. As an emergency field without a transmitter, there would be no answer until it would be made visually. He kept asking for the lights. He strained to see them in the darkened valleys. There were no lights at all.

In the distance he saw the mountains that surrounded Fremont Pass. They were level with him, which put him some four thousand feet above Leadville.

To the right Steve saw field lights come on. He slid toward them, circling. Sliding back the canopy he flipped the magnesium flare into the air. The split-cord around his finger ripped the cap from the tube and he flew out from under it. Behind him it spread its parachute and flared into the smoky brilliance. He marked the wind drift of the smoke, circled, and began letting down. At about forty feet he switched on his landing lamps, cutting a swath in the blackness. The plane jolted onto the runway.

Tom Baldwin was out to meet him as he taxied up to the little hangar. Steve cut the switches and leaped out of the cockpit onto the wing. "Gas it, Tom," he said.

"It'll have to be quick. I've been reading the radio, and the troopers'll be here anytime now. They got it when you called in for landing. That little red-nosed twerp in Idaho Springs must. have let 'em in on it."

The two men set to work. Steve ripped open the engine jacket and forced a quart of oil into the breather. Tom ground gasoline through the frost-bound pump until it spilled over the wings. Steve climbed back into the plane and retied Gina's hands. He got the engine turning over and then jumped back to the ground. He dug for his wallet and pressed the last hundred-dollar bill into Tom Baldwin's hand. A half-mile down the road were the lights of approaching cars.

"Here they come. Get out of here!"

"What will you tell them?"

"I'll think of something."

"Try this. Tell them you were robbed," Steve said, "it'd go easier with you."

"Yeah," Baldwin said, his face lighting up, "I guess it would."

Steve put his hand on the little man's shoulder, then swung with the other hand, a neat chopping left that dropped him like a sack of meal. He wrenched the hundred dollars from Baldwin's hand and jammed it into the mechanic's shirt pocket. Then he jumped onto the wing and dropped into the cockpit.

The Culver bit into the air at the north end of the strip just as the state troopers' cars ground to a halt before the hangar.

Some twenty minutes later Steve broke radio silence. He didn't tag the message or identify himself. He simply said, "Thanks, Tom."

The sun was high over the flat drylands of the Arkansas Valley when he put the Culver's wheels against the runway of Jake Morris' tiny airport.

CHAPTER THIRTY FIVE

Steve rolled the Culver to the service end of the strip at the end of his landing roll, wheeled it around, locked the brakes and slowed the laboring engine. Gina was awake and very sick. Her face alternately flushed and paled, and her shoulders trembled. Steve loosened the belts that had bound her arms and ankles to the seat. As the blood came back into her fingers she stifled a scream of pain.

"Move your hands, honey," Steve said. "Rub them, hard."

She looked at him with inexpressible loathing but did as she was told. Steve had retrieved her purse from behind the seat. He opened it and extracted the metal box that contained her supply of narcotics and the needle. He opened the four paper-wrapped bindles of heroin. She looked at him, her eyes pleading.

"I've got to have it, Steve. Please."

He didn't answer. His feet stomped on the brake pedals, and he opened the throttle until the engine was racing. He opened the door against the slipstream and let the air blast carry the white powder across the runway into the mesquite-covered drylands. Gina watched, not believing what was happening. The papers blew away. With his left hand still in the heavy flying glove, he snapped the glass tube of the hypodermic. The gleaming needle pressed against the metal instrument panel, bent, and then snapped. Steve slowed the engine, then cut the switches. The box that had held Gina's narcotics and equipment now contained only a teaspoon. He poured the shattered glass from his gloved hand back into the box and extracted the spoon, holding it out to her.

"This you can have," he told her.

Her nails bit down the side of his face, plowing bloody furrows until they broke off under his skin. She spit in his face.

He slapped her three times, slowly and deliberately. She wept. "It's got to be this way," he said. "But you can have a couple of these." He fished in the pocket of his flying jacket and pulled out the box of seconal. "We'll get some water in the hangar. Can you walk on those ankles? Are they still numb?"

She nodded. Her tear-stained face raised from the slump on her chest and she looked directly at him. "You're bleeding bad. I'm sorry."

He nodded, then got out of the plane, and went around to the other side to help her out. He pressed his handkerchief against the rips in his face. On the wing, she was swaying slightly. She half-fell into his arms. Supporting her as she took faltering steps, Steve led her into the hangar. Near the door was the jeep that served Jake as crash truck, emergency wagon, and towing tractor. Steve pulled the large first-aid suitcase from it and they went toward the office.

The sign on the door read "Back in ten minutes." Steve pushed open the unlocked door. Gina sagged into the swivel chair behind the desk and he gave her two seconal tablets, bringing a cup of water from the tiny washbowl in the corner of the office. Then he went back to the bowl and began to wash the blood off his face. It had streamed like a red cascade, splattering the shoulder of the jacket and giving the entire side of his face a smashed appearance. He winced against the sting of the soap, but continued to wash at the blood. He turned to get the first-aid kit. Gina was at his elbow with it. She pointed to a chair and he sat. She wiped out the furrows that her shattered nails had gouged. He stiffened against the corrosive astringent that staunched the blood. She packed the wounds with sulfa powder and applied tape and gauze strips. He looked up at her.

"I sure made a mess of your face."

"Yeah. I guess you did. You all right?"

"I feel awfully sick, but ..." she had a difficult time forming the words, "but I want to. I want to feel sick ... real sick."

"You mean you really want to kick the habit?"

"Yes. Steve—how could I have been suckered into this? How could I have been such a fool?"

He looked at her. It seemed as if her eyes were receding into the deep circles that had formed under them. Her face was puffy, distorted, and artificial. "It could happen to anybody," he began.

She interrupted, "But why? All my life people babied me ... I took advantage of it. I ... gloried in it. Nothing could touch me. Well, something has. I want to make it up to them ... and it's too late. I don't even know why you came to get me. Why didn't you just let me rot? I'm not worth it. I've hurt everybody. Now Carazzi will kill you for interfering."

"Carazzi won't kill anybody, not ever again." Steve told her briefly that the Denver combination was broken. He finished with the statement that Carazzi was through but he knew better. Men like Carazzi, twisted into accepting a premise of personal invulnerability and absolute power, were through only when they were dead. Carazzi was not dead. He was alive, hurt, and at large.

The seconal began to work on Gina then. She slipped into a half-waking state, cursing herself and her exalted sense of self-importance. Steve continued talking to her ... soothing and lulling her like a little child. She dropped into fitful sleep.

"Growing up isn't easy, little one," Steve mused to himself, "especially not the way you had to do it."

CHAPTER THIRTY SIX

Spring hit the arid Arkansas Valley, turning the irrigated belt into a softly rolling green amid the dusty grey of the drylands. Pack rats and prairie dogs nested in the increasing cover, and the baking earth was the cushion for torpid rattlesnakes shedding their skins. Here and there a lizard scampered, taking alarm at the rush of cattle and horses. The earth had come alive with the sun, holding promise of crops along the irrigation channels and grazing on the drylands.

Rogers Ashe himself did not push his herds to the dryland acreage this year. Friends of his were his horsemen, with old Ramon proudly but inefficiently in command. This was the team that moved the winter-lean herd out toward the broken range. Ramon, again the young vaquero, sat proudly in his old Mexican saddle and made broad sweeping gestures toward the grazing land. For him the fences did not exist, and rights of easement arranged by telephone had no place in the scheme of things. He lived in the Colorado of the turn of the century, when Rogers Ashe was a boy entering a man's world, and Ramon was the primo vaquero, the top-hand.

The softening of the earth softened some of the tension of the household. The men still went armed, and their women were not far from guns, but with no action relaxation had come. Steve was back. He had flown to Denver and completed his testimony, spending an interminable nine days before the grand jury. Steve was relieved to see that Vicki's bruises had yielded to time. Steve knew that he and Vicki would be able to work things out together. She stood fresh and clear-eyed, second in command to Steve's mother, who continued placid and imperturbable as a smooth stream. Gina, the first horrors of withdrawal over, was subdued and contrite, desperately eager to work and serve. Old Juana accepted expectancy without definition. She went on, preparing meals and bustling about the house, a sharp-leaded cuchillo along her thigh under the voluminous skirt; yet with Ramon no longer a posted sentry, she too found prime concern in the routine. The rifle-bell alarm was no. longer set.

Steve slouched on the edge of the watering trough while the black horse drank his fill. They had ridden to the fence line with the herd. The black snorted and lifted his head. Steve looked up to see his father approaching from the barn. The old man crossed the soft dust of the barn yard and sat beside his son, fumbling out his tobacco sack and expertly rolling a cigarette. He lighted it. It was half burned before he spoke.

"What happened in Denver this time?" His iron-grey eyes swept his son's face.

"They got out blanket indictments covering the whole syndicate. Denver never knew how big the rotten spot was. Anyhow, they got almost all of them."

"All but Carazzi." It wasn't a question.

"All but Carazzi." Steve lit a cigarette of his own from the pack in his shirt pocket. He scuffed his toe into the patch of clover that hugged the shade of the water tank. "Guys like Carazzi always seem to get away ... and the bigger ones. But I'll get Carazzi and I'll get the guy above him. I swear to ..."

"Son, I never did succeed in teaching you where a job ended, did I?" The old man's face clouded. He remembered the frightened little boy who had run home from the reservoir, shattered by his first experience with violent death and by the realization that he had stood by and done nothing to prevent it. It hadn't helped Steve when they found Warnie's body, his neck broken by the impact of the water. He knew then that he hadn't left Warnie to drown, but he also knew that without his prodding scream of "Yellow," the boy would be alive. Rogers Ashe had seen this knowledge drive Steve to attempt all kinds of feats to justify his existence. The old man had watched the self-castigation Steve had accepted as penance grow into a rigid core of pain and a compulsion to achieve. He saw his fourteen-year-old son become a driven man almost overnight, with no comfort in achievement and no belief in his own worth.

Rogers Ashe looked at his son, riveting Steve's attention with his eyes. "I never interfered with your business on any count, did I, son?" Steve nodded agreement. "You grew up knowing that your decisions were going to be your own. Generally speaking, they were pretty good decisions. But some were pretty poor—you lost a hundred head of stock on a range full of poison weed, you got thrown thirty-one times tryin' to break a killer horse, you blew a couple of thousand dollars on a no-count woman before you were even twenty years old." The old man paused as if waiting for contradiction. He rolled another cigarette and lighted it. Steve continued to watch.

"I think you're about to make another mistake, son. A worse mistake than all the others put together. You're a smart boy, but you're a hot-head, a real crusader. That isn't bad, not in itself, but you let your feelings run away with you and get the idea that you've got to get in and turn the screws that'll make the whole world run right again. Now," the old man went on, "I want to ask you just three questions."

"Shoot."

"The first one is: "What did you set out to do?"

"Get Vicki and Gina out from under Carazzi's whip."

"That you've done. The second question is how big is this organization that you're bucking?"

"I don't know. A lot of them, maybe nationwide. I know there's a man over Carazzi on the west coast somewhere."

"You had lots of publicity pictures taken when you were training to fight, didn't you?"

"Yeah."

"That wasn't my third question. I just threw that in to set up the third one. O.K., then, granting they would know you on sight and that there is a lot of them, just how far would you expect your luck to carry you if you went on? You're the man who wrecked millions of dollars' worth of their business for them, and any one of them could identify you with a picture." The old man smiled gently.

"But what am I supposed to do?" Steve was standing, a scowl cut into his face as he said the words. "Am I supposed to just sit on my butt and watch this thing grow? I know which way the wind blows. The way this outfit operates, they'll be back in Denver, setting the same kind of traps in six months."

"Maybe they will, son. Maybe they won't. You've taken care of the things you set out to do. You've got those two girls out of the mess they were in. You were lucky to do that. You've admitted the lucky breaks you had. You went into some things where you had to bank on luck. So far, it's come through for you. From here you know what the odds are. You won't have a prayer. The old man snorted. "You could draw eighteen inside straights in a row before you could whip the kind of odds you'd be up against. You took care of your own. You turned all the information you had over to the law and the grand jury. You've done what you can ... it's no personal crusade, Steve."

"I suppose you're right. But damn it, Dad, I don't believe in a half-way fight."

Rogers Ashe let his right hand make a lightning motion, drawing the pistol from the holster at his hip. A shot snapped. Forty feet away two pieces of elongated flesh had been a rattlesnake. The body writhed, and the shattered head skittered across the dust under the impact of death. The black horse moved a few feet away and stood there, drop-reined.

"Trying for the corn bin, I reckon," the old man said. "There's the proof of the very point I've been trying to make, son. Right now you're like that snake was. He's spring blind with shedding his skin. He's got only one sense to direct him how to strike, that's his hearing. If you went on with this business, you'd have just the chance that he had. He didn't see or hear where death came from. You wouldn't either. Even without a personal grudge, that outfit would kill you for the same reason I killed that snake —to keep him from making trouble."

Steve looked across at the body of the snake, still writhing under the suddenness of death. Then he looked back at his father. "I guess you're right," he said. "Besides that, I don't suppose I'll have to go looking for trouble. They'll probably come looking for me. I know Carazzi will."

"How are you so sure he won't give up and get into a hole somewhere?" the old man asked, rising.

"It's more than just a hunch, Dad. I know the guy. I've hurt him—he won't take that from anybody. He'll be here. He'll be here soon. He won't come blasting in, either. When he gets here he'll know exactly what he's doing. He probably knows every detail about our place by now. He's methodical, shrewd, everything a man ought to be, except that he's not a man, or a human being."

Rogers Ashe walked over to the body of the snake. He pulled the clasp knife from the pocket inside his boot and ripped the skin down. He hung the skin on the rail fence and bent to stab the body with his knife, carrying it to the small hog-pen in the shade of the barn. He tossed it in, and it was gone in a matter of seconds. He turned and came back to his son.

"He'll be here, then," Rogers Ashe said. It was a quiet, matter-of-fact tone.

CHAPTER THIRTY SEVEN

The black horse, still saddled, bent to crop at the little patch of clover as the two men began to saunter toward the house. The sun was hanging three-fourths of the way across the sky. Steve knew without glancing at his new watch that it was three o'clock. Rogers Ashe was known throughout the valley as a man of undeviating habits. A mid-afternoon coffee break was one of those habits, set while he was a boy on the rolling Virginia tidewater and scrupulously observed on the Colorado cattle spread for more than fifty years. Each day found a fifteen-minute period when work would wait. Coffee and baked goods were in order for all hands. It was eaten in the kitchen of the ranch house with Martha presiding. It was a time set apart, when ranch hands, the tenant farmer who raised the forage crops on the irrigated acres, and any passing neighbors sat at a common table as welcome guests.

Passing neighbors and friends had been few in recent weeks. No word had been spread, yet Rogers Ashe wore a gun. For thirty years in that section of Colorado, a rancher buckled on his gun only when he was expecting trouble. If he needed help, he could ask and receive it automatically If he said nothing, he was left alone until the gun was back on the peg inside the door of his home. For today's coffee, with Ramon taking the cattle to the grazing land and Will Hobbes, the tenant, busy at the floodgates, the family was alone.

Gina and Vicki sat across the table from Steve and his father. Juana had dropped her ample bulk into a chair at one end of the table, and Martha Ashe stood with her back to the door at the other end, using a broad spatula to cut generous pieces of pecan and molasses loaf. It was this way that Carazzi found them.

One moment the door was empty, and the next, Carazzi stood framed within it, the gun in his hand trained on a small spot in the center of Martha's back.

"Very cozy," he said quietly. "I'd hoped that I could find you all together."

Steve lunged to his feet. "Hold it!" Carazzi snapped. His voice bit into them like burned alum. He stepped into the room. "Now just as easy as you can, I want you all to stand up," he said. They rose and stood, silent. "You, grand-paw, drop that gun belt. Do it slow and easy."

The muscles of Rogers Ashe right thigh began to tense, the holster moving almost imperceptibly away from his leg. Slowly he lowered his hands toward his waist.

"Don't try it, Dad," Steve said quietly. The old man's hand slipped the buckle of the gun belt, and it dropped to the floor at his ankles.

"Now you, Steve!" Carazzi spoke with a special venom. Steve loosed the buckle of his gun belt and dropped it. "Step back from them, both of you!" Carazzi snapped.

The shock of realization had still not fully settled on them. Gina's eyes were widening with terror and hatred. Vicki had gasped when she had heard his voice breaking into the afternoon chat, but she had made no sound since. Martha Ashe still stood at the head of the table, imperturbable as ever. Old Juana looked from one to the other of the family, then turned her mahogany mestiza, face to Carazzi. Her hand crept toward a fold in her skirt where a pocket could have been.

She whipped the knife out and threw it in a single motion. Carazzi fired. The knife raked his left arm. Juana sagged against the table, clutching at her side. Rogers Ashe and Steve had simultaneously jumped forward, but the gun in Carazzi's hand swung back to cover them. They froze in their tracks. Martha Ashe came calmly around, the table.

"Don't move!" Carazzi spit at her.

She threw him a glance of infinite scorn, and continued to move to Juana. Helping the old woman to a chair, she ripped the heavy cotton blouse away from the wound. She pulled clean linen napkins from the old silver ring-stand in the center of the table and began to bind Juana's wound. Carazzi stared at them, uncomprehendingly.

"The great charity of the Ashe family," he sneered. "If I had the time I think I'd be sick." His voice had slithered over the word and left it unclean. "Charity ... and strength in time of trouble. Rogers Ashe and family, so damned predictable with their generous help."

Steve felt the cut of the words. "How did you ..." he began.

"Get here? I have the reputation of the Ashe family to thank for that, also. Known throughout the countryside." His face let the smirk stray into a sardonic grin. "You think it was an accident that I'm here in time for coffee? All the other neighbors have a standing invitation, and since you've been my neighbors for two weeks, I thought I'd drop in." His face hardened again. "Since I got away from Denver I've been in Las Animas. Nice friendly little town. Vito was able to hear plenty about Rogers Ashe ... even about the afternoon coffee break. I've timed you for three days, watching from out there." His free hand gestured toward the drylands.

"How'd you get away from Brook Forest?"

"Vito took me on his back when that plane showed up. I suppose that was you?"

"Yes."

"Clever boy, Vito. We went out the road in the car tracks and watched the fight from the woods across the road. You cost me a lot of good boys."

"After that?"

"We stayed at someone else's place for two days, then got on skis we found there."

"Until you could get a car and get to Las Animas?"

"Until I could get to you."

"I suppose you just waited until I got home?"

"That's right. I wanted to talk. I wanted to see you squirm, knowing it was coming and not knowing when. I've had plenty of chances at you. I could have nailed you with a rifle this morning when you rode to the fence with the herd, but that wouldn't do. I want you to know where it's coming from, and I want it to come slow." Carazzi's face was a grey mask. He moved on into the room.

"Too bad you can't stake me down over a green bamboo shoot. That wouldn't be enough, though, would it?" Steve was puzzled at the detachment of his voice, almost as if it didn't belong to him.

"My way should prove enough. Now let's talk. I've got plenty of things to say." Carazzi limped across the room, his injured foot putting screw-threads of pain around his mouth with each jolting step. "This foot is something you gave me," he said, "I want you to know how it feels." He fired, and the bullet tore into the floor beside Steve's foot. He fired another shot, and another.

"Your shooting's mighty poor," Rogers Ashe said quietly.

Carazzi swung the gun back to a level with Rogers Ashe's belly. "Maybe it is, old man," he said, "but I'll have lots of chances." He bent and scooped up Rogers Ashe's heavy sixgun. Holding it in his left hand, he quickly pumped out the remaining shell from the banker's special in his right. It punctured Steve's boot like a lightning stroke with an awl. A tiny well of blood began to appear on the surface of the dusty leather. Steve's face paled with the shock.

"As for you," the olive-skinned man said, swinging his gaze to Vicki and transferring the sixgun to his right hand after he had pocketed the little belly gun, "you could have had the moon, just by asking for it. You walked out. You'll get a chance to walk out again—just as far as the hog-pen. That's the place for a pig to die."

Vicki colored, looking at him. "Remember I'm one pig who couldn't stomach your kind of filth."

He swung the gun toward her again, his finger tightening on the trigger. Then he calmed, and went icy cold. He turned to Gina. "You!" he said. "How's your habit? Been able to get a fix lately?" He fumbled in his left coat pocket and tossed a box on the table. "Give yourself a jolt," he said.

"No!"

"Do it now," he purred, "or I'll kill all of you."

"You wouldn't!"

"I've got reason to kill your sister and her boyfriend. The rest of you can live. If you don't try to make trouble. Now give yourself that jolt—right now."

Slowly Gina opened the kit. She mixed the powder in the shell of the spoon, using a few drops of water from a glass on the table.

"How do I know it isn't poison?" she asked.

"You don't. It might be prussic acid, but you'll take it anyhow."

She inserted the tip of the needle into the bell of the spoon and withdrew the plunger slowly. The milky colored mixture climbed up into the glass barrel of the syringe.

"You're a miserable, stinking ..." Steve began.

Carazzi wheeled and blasted three shots from the six-gun. Steve reeled, clutching at his shoulder and sagged to the floor.

What happened then was like lightning. Gina's hand contacted on the syringe plunger, pumping a stream of milky fluid into Carazzi's face. Wildly he fired twice more, the bullets furrowing the table beside her. Rogers Ashe went for him. The little man wheeled to meet the onslaught and pulled the trigger. The hammer fell on the spent cartridge Rogers Ashe had used in killing the snake. Carazzi clubbed the gun and brought it down hard across the old man's head. Vicki dove for the gun belt Steve had dropped. She came up with the gun, firing before it had even cleared the floor. Carazzi broke and ran from the door. She scrambled up and ran after him. He reached the barn lot.

The great black stallion felt the sudden impact of a man scrambling into the saddle and was away. Vicki emptied the gun after him.

Carazzi and the horse had made perhaps three hundred yards when Steve made it to the door. He let out a piercing whistle. The black horse stopped in his tracks. Carazzi was thrown headlong from the saddle and the horse began to trot back to the house.

When Rogers Ashe began to stir, and Steve knew his father was alive, Steve reloaded the old man's sixgun and staggered out the door. He hauled himself into the saddle of the black and rode out into the mesquite. It was a long ten minutes later before the women waiting at the house heard shots ... four quick shots.

Carazzi lay across the pommel of the saddle as Steve came back, slumped forward across the body. Carazzi's coat sleeve was ripped open, jagged splinters of bone where his elbow should have been.

"He'd crawled off into the brush," Steve said, "right into a nest of rattlesnakes. That's what I shot. That's why it took me so long to find him. Better get a doctor."

Vicki caught Steve as he slumped from the saddle. Martha Ashe helped to lower him to the ground, and with unsuspected strength the two women carried him to the house.

Carazzi's body slid from the back of the huge stallion, the horse moving away from the rake of the man's feet down his shoulder. The movement rolled the body.

Gina Marotti stood and looked down at the face of Mario Carazzi. He lay dead, face up on the Colorado earth he had sought to ravage. His broken forearm was twisted at a weird angle. She reached out with her foot and straightened it. The inside surface bore the puncture marks of rattlesnake fangs like hypodermic punctures over the main artery.

Inside the house, Steve felt a sense of release. In spite of the pain of his wounds, he was at rest for the first time within his memory. Now that Carazzi was dead, it seemed to Steve that he would have no further need to crusade.

Vicki was bending over him, weeping softly. He reached out and took her hand.

THE END

Made in the USA
Middletown, DE
11 September 2023

38348333R00120